# Mystery at Burr Oak
## A Dog Named Wang

## Karen Carr

ISBN 978-1-61225-322-0

Copyright © 2015 Karen Carr
All Rights Reserved

This is a work of fiction. Names, characters, businesses, places, events and incidents are either the products of the author's imagination or used in a fictitious manner. Any resemblance to actual persons, living or dead, or actual events is purely coincidental.

No part of this publication may be reproduced in any form or stored, transmitted or recorded by any means without the written permission of the author.

Published by Mirror Publishing
Milwaukee, WI 53214
www.pagesofwonder.com

Printed in the USA

I wrote this story to honor my mother, Beulah Fields. The character of Dotty is patterned after Mom in three ways. First, Dotty was my mother's nickname; second, she used idioms and aphorisms quite a bit in her everyday language; and third, Mom had a dog named Wanger Doops who would howl when she sang the Wang, Wang Blues (a song popular in 1920.) Dotty's other characteristics came from my own imagination as well as the rest of the book.

# Chapter One

The sleepy Midwestern river town of Gannon Ridge sat nestled in the hillside overlooking the Mississippi River. Giant oak trees covered the sloping streets, providing a cooling shade in the heat of midsummer. Limestone walls lined the Wisconsin side of the nearby river, making it a gorgeous scenic backdrop. The trees were dressed in a vibrant green while the grassy hillsides resembled beds of emeralds. Gannon Ridge, Iowa was an old river town founded by its namesake, Col. Thomas Gannon, who had served in the Civil War. The annual Col. Tom Days had become the town's memorial tribute to Gannon and his contributions to the town throughout the years. Not to mention just a way for the people to celebrate and have a good time. Col. Tom Days, held in the middle of July, was the social event of the year. People joined in from miles around. Venders came from all over Iowa and even Wisconsin.

It was into the midst of one of these celebrations that Penelope Powers drove into town. Penny, as she was known back in New York where she was from, was amazed at the beauty of the surrounding country. Just seeing the Midwest countryside was amazing. There was not much green to be seen where she lived in New York.

It was with eager anticipation that she'd made this trip: the first time she'd been this far west. As she maneuvered her gray Honda CRV through the throng of the town's folk, she keenly felt the excitement of the community.

A banner spanned the main street touting "Col. Tom Days –July 12-14". Booths displaying crafts, food items, and art lined the Town Square. The community band played in the gazebo in the center of the Square. Church groups provided home cooked meals in the tents. A booth was set up for the Girls Scouts to sell their cookies. The Gannon Ridge high school pep club had a dunk tank. The girl's 4H club was giving free cooking demonstrations and area politicians threaded their way through the crowds, handing out their brochures. Gannon Ridge was all decked out and in a festive mood.

*This is so much different than in the big city. I just know this was the right thing to do.* She leaned forward eagerly on the seat of her Honda.

Pulling into the crowded parking lot of the Gannon Ridge Inn, Penny was thankful that her lawyer had convinced her to reserve a room there ahead of time. With this crowd she was sure it would have been difficult to find lodging.

Penny stepped out of the Honda and slowly stretched her legs. She had been traveling for quite some time now and she felt a little stiff. She brushed the crumbs off of her jeans. *That's what happens when I eat in the car. I really am a sloppy eater.*

Grabbing her purse and locking her vehicle, Penny entered the Gannon Ridge Inn to register. Looking around, she observed a warm atmosphere, decorated in a nautical theme.

"Welcome to Gannon Ridge and welcome to the Gannon Ridge Inn," was the friendly greeting from the man behind the desk. He was slender, maybe in his late 50's with thinning red hair, and a red mustache peppered with white. "You must be Penelope Powers."

Penny nodded. "How did you know my name?" She looked curiously at the man behind the desk.

"Simple," was the reply. "Only one empty room left and it's reserved for Penelope Powers. Besides, Burr Oak needs some work before you can stay there, so we knew you'd be staying here. It's the only overnight accommodation in Gannon Ridge." He thrust out his hand, "I'm Joe Freeman, owner and manager of this here establishment."

Noticing Penny's expression, Joe said, "You'll get used to everyone knowing all about you, Ms. Powers. That's the way it is in a small town. The whole town's been all a buzz about the city gal who's coming to fix up Burr Oak. Hasn't been anyone living there since old Harry Powers moved to the city five years ago." Joe paused and looked closer at Penny. "As a matter of fact, you kind of favor Harry."

Penny smiled. "Thank you, Mr. Freeman. Yes, he and my father looked a lot alike and I "kind of favor" my father."

"I can sure see that. And you just call me Joe. Everyone in Gannon Ridge does."

"Thank you, Joe," she smiled. "And please, call me Penny."

While Penny signed in, Joe gave her a rundown of what was going on for the celebration in town. "Col. Tom was the man that founded this here town. Town loved him, and they loved his family, too. But none of them left anymore. Last living Gannon descendant sold Burr Oak to Harry Powers way back when Harry was a young man."

"That's interesting. I didn't realize that Burr Oak belonged to the Gannon family."

"Yup. Col. Tom built Burr Oak back before the Civil War. He was a real hero to our town. Still is. Did a lot for the town and it's lasted down through the years. Real friend to the community, he was. Gannon Ridge was a booming river port back then. Commerce on the river was what made it grow. Course now, the docks are mainly for pleasure boats. The Col. Tom docks here. It's a replica of an old steamship. It's now a dinner cruise ship."

"What did Tom Gannon do for a living?"

"Oh, he was a river merchant. Owned a whole fleet of barges that hauled everything from grain to furs down to New Orleans. Made a lot of money for his family, but he shared his wealth with the town, too. He built the school, the bank and several other buildings on Main Street. Our town is listed on the National Register."

"The town has restored several of the buildings Col. Tom built on Main Street. The Gannon Ridge Inn here was one of them. And they are all made of limestone. Col. Tom mined the stone from the nearby quarry to build all the buildings."

*This town is sure full of history and friendly people,* thought Penny.

"You can hear her blow from here."

With a start, Penny's thoughts returned to the present and asked, "I'm sorry, who blows?"

"The whistle. You can hear the whistle blow every time the Col. Tom pulls out from the dock," said Joe.

Joe handed Penny the key to room 22. "If there's anything you need, you be sure and let me know."

Penny thanked Joe and went out the front door to her Honda. After pulling around to her room, she removed two of the bags. The Honda was packed full; both inside and on top but the rest of the things were for Burr Oak. The remainder of her belongings would come by moving van from the city as soon as she gave them the word.

After freshening up a bit in the bathroom, which included drawing her long hair into a ponytail, Penny changed her jeans and shirt and left the room, placing the key in her jeans pocket. She decided the celebration would be a good way to get to know the people of Gannon Ridge since it seemed that just about every one of them must be there on Main Street.

Since it was nearing the evening mealtime, Penny opted to find a restaurant instead of one of the venders in the park. It was pretty warm, the Midwestern July heat was almost stifling and she thought it would be nice to set in an air-conditioned building while she ate. Just down the block, Penny espied a sign advertising that Meg's Diner was open, so she headed there. As she entered Meg's, Penny noted that there were not a lot of customers for such a busy time in the town. The sign just inside the door noted that the "supper" special was Chicken Alfredo.

A man in a white apron handed her a menu and seated her in a booth next to the window. As she slid into the booth, Penny commented to him that business seemed slow in light of the crowd outside.

"Oh, that's because they're all eating outside. There are booths in the Town Park that sell hot dogs, hamburgers, chicken—all kinds of food. But I still stay open during most of the doings." He pause, "Welcome to Meg's Diner. I'm Meg and you must be Penelope Powers."

Penny was astonished. "I'm amazed. Does everyone here know who I am?"

"Pretty much. Small town, not much gets past us here."

"Did you say your name was Meg? " Penny asked, as she'd suddenly comprehended how he had introduced himself.

"Yeah," he answered sheepishly. "Been called Meg since I was knee-high to a grasshopper. Real name's Howard Meggers, Jr. Don't much care for Howard, and Meg just kind of stuck from when I was a kid."

"Well, Meg, I'm pleased to meet you. But please call me Penny.

Now, what have you got on the dinner menu? I'm starving."

"Not serving dinner now. It's supper time."

"Oh," said Penny. "Where I come from dinner is the evening meal; lunch is the noon meal."

Meg grunted, "Yup, I've heard that. Around here lunch is what you take in a sack or something to tide you over in the afternoon when you're too hungry to wait for supper."

"Well, I'll be," said Penny, and with that said, she ordered the 'supper special.'

Penny asked Meg about the activities outside in the town square and about Burr Oak; she found that her excitement was growing as she anticipated getting to see Burr Oak for herself. As Meg continued talking, Penny dreamily glanced out the window near the table where she saw a rather large, brown dog. He had a friendly look in his eyes. He continued to look at Penny; his large, brown eyes seemed to be asking Penny a question. Strange. Wonder what he is thinking.

"Can you tell me how to get to Burr Oak?"

"Sure," said Meg as he placed her plate in front of her. "You just take Main Street out in front here and go north until you are out of town, cross the bridge and turn right at the first intersection. Then the road winds up the hill and goes right to Burr Oak. Can't miss it."

Penny looked again out the window, but the big, brown dog was no longer there. Penny found that she was a little disappointed. She turned back to the conversation with Meg.

"Is Burr Oak limestone?" Penny asked, remembering what Joe had said about so many buildings being made out of limestone. She had thought with the name of Burr Oak it would be made out of oak.

"Oh, it's limestone on the outside, but it's all oak on the inside. It's named for the type of oak trees outside the house. Wait until you see it! Beautiful inside and out. Been setting empty for three years. Hard telling what it will look like inside. It'll need some fixing up, but it's great stuff to work with. They don't make 'em like that anymore." Meg suddenly seemed quite enthusiastic when the subject was Burr Oak.

"Have you always lived in Gannon Ridge, Meg?"

"No, moved here a couple of years ago and opened up the diner."

# Chapter Two

Penny finish eating, and bidding Meg goodbye and thanking him for the information, she headed down to the Town Square to get in on the evening's celebrating. She noticed with interest the many shops that lined the square. The Stitchery, Books and More Books, Toys Galore, Coffee, Tea and Thee, The Sweet Shoppe, A Quilter's Attic, and Gifts and Crafts were just a few of the small shops around the square.

The music had changed to a country band and was playing country western music. Penny found herself humming along as she made the rounds of the booths and venders. She purchased a sack of kettle corn (her first ever) and was pleasantly pleased with the sweet/salty flavor.

The lady at the kettle corn booth smiled as she watched the pleased expression cross Penny's face.

"I knew you'd like it," she said.

"I do. It's a nice flavor."

"Welcome to Gannon Ridge," she said holding out her hand. "I'm Linda Booth, hence the sign, the Booth's Booth."

Penny smiled as she looked at the sign and shook the extended hand. "Pleased to meet you. I'm Penny Powers, or did you know that already?"

Linda laughed. "Well, I figured it must be you. Are you getting a lot of that?"

"Yes," said Penny. "But that's okay. It's kind of nice. You don't get that much in the city."

"Good. Don't want to scare you away. But listen, I have to get back to work here. My husband, Jerry, took his supper break and I'm getting kind of busy. Here's my business card with my phone number on it. Call any time after this celebration is over and we'll get together for coffee."

Penny took the card and also gave Linda her cell phone number. "Nice meeting you, Linda. I look forward to getting together."

Penny made several purchases at the various craft booths. This was really fun and the people were very friendly. She could hardly wait until she could begin placing these things in her new home. She was happy to have made Linda's acquaintance, too. It was nice to know she had made a friend.

Penny sat on a park bench near the gazebo while she munched on the kettle corn and listened to the band. The evening was beautiful and she was really enjoying herself. She found herself tapping her foot to the beat. Penny put the sack of kettle corn down next to her on the bench so that she could look at some of the purchases she'd made. She had purchased several garden-related items. *Of course, I might be jumping the gun a bit. Maybe there isn't even room for an herb garden at Burr Oak.* But she felt that anything that was called an "estate" certainly must be big enough to have a garden. And if there wasn't she'd just have to create one.

The big, brown dog, who had peered in Meg's window at Penny, came up to her park bench. He sniffed at the sack of kettle corn and at the same time, kept an eye on her. Still watching her, he began to eat some of the kernels that had fallen from the sack.

"Are you hungry, big fella?"

The dog stopped crunching and seemed to hold his breath. *Maybe he thinks I'm going to take it away from him.*

"Go ahead, boy. You can eat it."

Penny heard a high-pitched bark. The dog also heard the bark. She followed his glance over to where a small white poodle stood barking. When Penny turned back to the dog beside her, he was gone. *Along with my bag of kettle corn! I do wish he'd stick around though. Oh well, he had seemed hungry.*

The band had stopped playing and the night's festivities were nearing an end. Penny decided it was time to head back to the motel and she reached for her sack of kettle corn, but remembered that it was gone. *I hope he is enjoying that kettle corn!*

The evening wore on and Penny began to feel exhausted. As she walked back to the Inn, she thought about the pleasant drive from the city. The scenery had been so beautiful. The education of rural life was enlightening. Such a difference from living in an apartment in a large New England city. Not that the apartment was by any means a dinky one. In fact, it was the penthouse and it was really in both her name and her father's.

Penny sighed as she thought of her father, wishing he were here with her. He would have enjoyed this as much as she did. William Powers had been the CEO of a large and very successful company, one he had formed as a young man. Her mother had passed away when she was ten years old, so it had been just Penny and her dad for quite some time. Her paternal grandmother had stayed with them, caring for Penny while she was younger.

When Penny was older, she had worked in her father's company, too. When her father retired, Penny took over some of his duties. The vice president became the new CEO and Penny became the vice president. Penny found she did not want the position, which her father had held for so many years. However, he still entertained many business contacts. In that way, her father was able to keep his hand and interest alive in his company. Penny continued as her father's hostess. Their home was getting too big for them at this point since her grandmother had passed away when she was a senior in high school, so eventually they sold the house and moved into the penthouse of a large apartment building.

Then suddenly, her father suffered a severe stroke, which left him paralyzed on the left side. Penny made the decision to leave the family company and stay home to take care of her invalid father. He was wheelchair-bound and other than not having the use of his left arm and leg, he was otherwise in good health.

Penny and her father traveled up and down the East Coast. They did things they'd never had the time for when he was still involved in the company. She and her father had some very special times: more father-daughter bonding than they had had time for in years.

For five years, her father lived in such a way until another stroke finally took him from her. But during the last three years of her father's life, they'd shared their lives with another family member, Harry Powers, her father's brother. Harry lived in Gannon Ridge and had been to the city to visit only a half dozen times that Penny could remember.

They'd not heard much from Harry, just the usual Christmas greetings and occasional letters in between. So it was a complete surprise when a telegram arrived one day from Harry, saying:

> *"On way to city with bag and baggage. Arrive noon Wednesday. Please meet at airport?????"*

Penny supposed that the question marks meant he really was asking, not telling. As it turned out, Harry was a wonderful friend. His character and personality were very much like that of his brother. So it was very easy for them to ask him to stay with them, permanently.

Though he never said as much, Penny assumed that Harry was lonely and that he knew both his and his brother's time was nearing an end. He wanted to be a part of his family again. Penny for one was glad that Harry had come to live with them. When her father passed away, it meant a lot to have Harry there and she believed that he too was thankful that he had come and been a part of his brother's life before he was gone.

Although both Penny and Harry still owned stock in the company, they no longer had any part in the day-to-day business. But Penny's father had been well off, you might say, and with both of them still owning stock in the company, they didn't want for anything.

Then recently Uncle Harry had suddenly suffered a heart attack and passed away. Penny was devastated. She had really come to love her uncle and to enjoy his presence. She would miss him very much. He was Penny's last remaining relative. That fact caused her much sadness. She really was alone in the world now.

In his will, Harry had left Penny his remaining stock. What had been a total surprise was that he also willed her his beloved Burr Oak. It had been a surprise because for one thing, Penny had assumed that Uncle Harry had sold it when he moved to the city. Many times Uncle Harry had talked fondly of Burr Oak. Penny had never seen it, except for one picture he had, and in her imagination, as he would tell stories about Burr Oak and the town of Gannon Ridge and the people who lived there.

Finding herself without her loved ones and all alone in that big apartment, Penny wanted to do something different, something exciting. She had no desire to go back to work in the company, though she certainly could have. Penny had lived that life and its rat race, and she wanted a change. Now was the time to do it. She was young and she knew what she wanted to do and she had the means to do it. She had a plan. She called her lawyer and asked him make the necessary arrangements for her to leave the city and move to Gannon Ridge. Burr Oak was calling to her, thanks to the stories of Uncle Harry.

Needless to say, Penny's lawyer thought she'd gone off the deep end and he tried several times to talk reason with her. "At least go out there first and see what it is like," he counseled. "You have no idea what you might be getting yourself into. That big old house could be a wreck. It could turn out to be a money pit"

"Well, that doesn't seem to be a problem for me, does it?" Penny laughed.

Penny's mind was made up, however. She had spent many hours those last few years listening to Uncle Harry's stories of Gannon Ridge and Burr Oak. She felt like she could picture the big house without ever having laid eyes on it. She had only seen the picture of the house, which had been hanging in Harry's room. Penelope Powers was starting a new life and she felt the thrill of excitement as she had pointed her Honda CRV west, leaving her New England home. She almost felt like a pioneer woman leaving her home behind and heading west into the unknown. If they could do it, so could she.

Penny was in her late twenties, attractive with long brown hair and big brown eyes. She was a slender 5 foot 7. She believed that nothing happened out of coincidence, but that everything happened for a purpose, designed and created by a Higher Power, namely God. So she was anxious to see what future her Heavenly Creator had planned for her.

This morning Penny had driven along on rural roads in her newly purchased Honda. As she'd neared Gannon Ridge, she decided it was perfect timing and accepted it as God's will. She had made arrangements to dispose of the apartment, put her furniture in storage, and had packed up and moved out here sight unseen. She was ready to start her new life.

The lawyer told Penny that the house had stood empty all of those three years, so it was hard telling what it really looked like, as Meg had said. But he understood that Burr Oak had been quite a show place in its day. It probably would take quite a bit to fix it up, but Penny had money and her inheritance, so that would not be a problem.

Anyway, here she was in Gannon Ridge now, burning her bridges behind her. There was no turning back now. No place to go if she did go back. And tomorrow she would go to see her new home. It was a little scary, really. But she was craving excitement and adventure, wasn't she? And this was certainly one way to get it. Though some of her acquaintances in the city told her she was foolish to give it all up and move to a hick town somewhere in the Midwest, she was still adamant about moving there.

As Penny let herself into her room at the Inn, she had the distinct feeling of being watched. She turned around peered into the shadows, but saw nothing. *Hmmm, guess I'm just tired. I'd better call it a day.* Penny did not see the brown dog in the shadows watching her.

# Chapter Three

As the sunrise brought a beautiful pink glow to the eastern sky with the river in the foreground, Penny headed down to Meg's Diner for breakfast. Penny was impressed by the view. There was no smog!

"Top of the morning to you, Penny." Meg greeted her.

"And the same to you, Meg," Penny said shyly. She hadn't quite gotten used to calling a man 'Meg.' "It's a fine looking morning. Are the sunrises always this beautiful?"

"Well now, as long as the sky is clear it'll always look this way. Guess I'm just used to them. I don't stop to think about it. But you're right. Does look mighty fine."

"My, I don't think I would ever get used to that sight. Can you see the sunrise at Burr Oak?"

His eyes twinkled with excitement, "Guess you can see it both rise and set!"

"I am so excited about seeing the place I'm ready to go now. Could you a fix me a cold sack lunch to-go? I want to eat my lunch there while I'm cleaning," she said, mindful of the distinction between lunch and dinner.

Meg gave her the lunch and she settled her bill. "See you around, Penny."

As Penny settled her bill, she saw movement out of the corner of her eye. Turning she saw that it was the same dog she had seen the night before. Again, he looked so friendly and such a beautiful dog.

"Thank you, Meg," she paused at the door. "There he is again!"

"There's who again?"

"That dog, by the door."

"What dog?" asked Meg, seeing no dog.

Penny was beginning to think she was imagining things. "Well, there was a dog there, but I guess he is gone now."

"Probably just a stray," Meg said.

After leaving the diner, Penny walked to the town square. Joe had told her that on Sunday morning, the Community Church would be holding services in the park. Penny got her Bible from her room and made her way to a seat in the park. People were friendly and greeted her with enthusiasm. Linda Booth and her husband, Jerry came just then and seeing Penny, they came and sat next to her.

"Hi, Penny. So good to see you this morning. It's a lovely Lord's day, isn't it?"

Penny agreed whole heartedly.

"This is my husband, Jerry. Jerry, this is Penny Powers. She is Harry's niece."

"Nice to meet you, Penny," Jerry said reaching past Linda to shake her hand. "Welcome to Gannon Ridge."

"Thank you very much. I am already in love with Gannon Ridge."

As the service started, Penny discovered she had another friend on her side opposite Linda. Penny glanced over at Linda but she had not seen the dog. Penny's hand slipped down and she stroked the dog's head. She scratched behind his left ear and he seemed to enjoy it immensely.

Penny saw a toddler in the row ahead, turn to see the dog. And so did the dog. He immediately got up and left. *Guess he doesn't like children.*

Following the worship service, Penny said her goodbyes to Linda and Jerry and made her way back to the Inn and got into her Honda. She was more than ready to go check out Burr Oak –her new home. Following the directions Meg had provided, Penny made her way through town and up the ridge road.

There it was. Burr Oak. There was an enormous stone house overlooking the river with a magnificent view from the wrap-around porch both to the east and the west. Meg was right. Her imagination had not quite prepared her for such a large place. Her uncle had really not done it justice in his descriptions. Neither had his picture that hung on the wall in his room at the penthouse.

Penny parked the Honda in front of the big house and ascended the steps to the veranda. The main entrance faced the south. What a wonderful old house. Penny was simply awestruck. Big, my goodness, it was big! She took the key from her purse and unlocked the front door. She peered into the front entryway.

Cobwebs and dust blanketed everything. But the furniture was all covered with dust cloths. It wasn't nearly as bad as she had envisioned it might be though. Penny walked into the large entryway and turned to the room at the left. It appeared to be a parlor with glass doors opening out onto the west veranda. A magnificent limestone fireplace stood at one end. Even with the coat of dust she could see that the woodwork around the doors and the windows was a beautiful oak. Even the stone fireplace supported an oak trim around it.

In the center of the room was a large covered object. Penny went to it and pulled the cover off. She gasped at the sight before her-the most beautiful grand piano she had ever had the privilege to see. Because it was covered, the dust had not touched it. Perhaps the changing weather may have caused some problems though.

Penny lifted the cover and struck a chord. Well, at least it sounded like a piano. It was such a beautiful instrument; it would be a shame if it couldn't be restored. She surely intended to do her best to see that it was done, no matter the cost.

Leaving the parlor, Penny crossed the entryway. On the right side was another large room. She entered the room and discovered it was an enormous dining room. This room also had a fireplace at one end of the room just like the parlor.

On the north side of the dining room was a swinging door, which she discovered led to the kitchen. On each side of the swinging door were large brass push plates with ornate designs etched around the word "PUSH." And the kitchen, well, to say this room was extremely large would be an understatement. It had a large pantry, a commercial stove, and a walk-in freezer. The appliances were all present with doors standing open. Penny had noticed that both the dining room and the kitchen had east windows, to see the sunrise! From the windows in the parlor, the sunset could be enjoyed.

On the west side of the kitchen was another door that led into the north end of the entryway, near the wide, winding stairway. "How magnificent," Penny said aloud.

Behind the stairway was a large oak door and upon opening it, she discovered it must be the library or den. A large oak desk stood in the center of the room. It was indeed the focal point of the room. The walls of the library were covered with empty bookshelves. On closer inspection, Penny discovered that several boxes were stacked in one corner along the wall. The boxes appeared to be full of books. She was ecstatic that the books were still there and appeared to be in such good shape except for a little dust on the boxes. Well, actually, a lot of dust. At least they were in the boxes, which she had looked into. *Wonderful*. Penny was a book lover. The desk was gorgeous and looked to be in pristine condition.

A utility room led into the kitchen by another door. A small suite of rooms was adjacent to the parlor. It included a sitting room, bedroom and bathroom, with a tiny kitchenette. Uncle Harry had used this apartment as his own living quarters. It had that homey lived-in look to it. Penny was just closing the door when she heard a sound come from the library. She went back to that room and opened the door.

"Oh my goodness! It's you again!"

There in the library, was the same big, brown dog that Penny had seen from the diner and again at the park. "Hey, you. Come here. How did you get in here? Here, big fella. Nice doggie, come here."

*Well, this isn't going to work. I need some food to coax him out.* Penny went back to the entryway to retrieve her purse and bag that she had set on the table just inside the front door. Opening the bag, she took out part of a sandwich that was in the lunch sack Meg had made for her. She returned to the library "Now, here you go. Here's something for you to…"

The dog was gone. There was no sign of him, although there was a multitude of paw prints in the dusty floor. He could not have left the library or Penny would have seen him. But it was a fact. He was not there now.

"I wonder if I am more tired that I had thought. My imagination must be playing tricks on me," Penny murmured.

Shrugging off that thought, Penny decided it was time to investigate the upstairs. The wide stair led to the upstairs hallway. There were so many doors opening into the hallway that she was amazed. Penny was almost breathless with the possibilities that this house brought to her. She had secretly been nursing that idea that she would be able to create a Bed and Breakfast here, and after seeing all those bedrooms, she knew the possibilities were definitely good. The kitchen was nearly industrial-size; the dining room was large enough to have several small tables or one banquet-style table for guests, and the parlor would be great for all sorts of entertainment for guests.

The grand piano would really be great for guest entertainment. The veranda or porch that wound around three sides of the house would be great for guests to enjoy both sunrise and sunset. And the view in between looking out over the Mississippi River was worth the look too.

Penny left the house by way of the back door next to the apartment. What she found out back was what she had hoped with all her heart she would find. It was a formal garden complete with a gazebo in the center and good-sized herb garden. She found oregano, tarragon, thyme and mint in the tangle. Of course, most of the perennial herbs were growing out of control, but that wasn't anything a little transplanting and TLC wouldn't cure. Then she could add a few annual herbs to complete the garden. Next to the garden was a large 2-story carriage house. It was in great shape for such an old building. On the south side of the carriage house was a small-attached greenhouse.

*This just keeps getting better and better*, Penny thought joyfully.

Penny stood out in the circle drive and viewed the house (manor was more like it) and was absolutely speechless. It was more than she could ever have hoped for. And she was anxious to get started. So she went to the Honda and retrieved brooms, mops, rags, a pail and other cleaning paraphernalia.

Penny's lawyer had called ahead to have the utilities turned on, so that she would have no problem when she began her cleaning. Both the water and electricity were turned on, but the phone wouldn't be hooked up until Monday. Fortunately, she had a cell phone. She had a lot of work to do so she'd best get busy.

Deciding to start first with the apartment, Penny brought in her cleaning supplies from the Honda and began with the bedroom. Next she cleaned the bathroom. She found a stepladder in the utility room off of the kitchen. As Penny was bringing the ladder back to the suite, she peeked in the library to see if the dog was there. *Nope. Didn't think so.*

Penny went into the apartment and began cleaning the walls in the bedroom and there he was-on the bed! "How do you do that?" she asked him. Of course, she didn't expect him to answer. But he did look quizzically at her with just ever so slight a tilt to his head. And she was even sure he had raised one eyebrow.

He did not have a collar, so evidently he didn't belong to anyone. "Well, dog, you know what? There's room for you too in this big house and I do need some company, so you can stay." Penny thought he looked pleased. She approached him carefully. You never know if it is safe to approach a strange dog or not. Putting her hand behind his head, she gave one ear a scratch. The dog appeared to enjoy it. In fact, he enjoyed it so much if he had been a cat, he would have been purring.

Penny though he was probably a lab, due to his light brown color, probably a yellow or golden lab.

"Wonder what I should call you. I can't just keep calling you dog. I'll have to think a while on it."

The dog watched her while she began cleaning the walls, his head following her around the room as she cleaned the windows. This was the only room that didn't have a sunrise or sunset view as it was on the north side of the house. "Oh, well. At least the guests would have the good views," she told the dog.

It was lunchtime and Penny had certainly worked up an appetite. She retrieved her purse and removed the sack lunch and thermos. She sat down in the sitting room and began eating. The dog had now left the bedroom and came out into the sitting room. He climbed up on the leather sofa where she was sitting and looked hungrily at her. "Well, there are two big sandwiches. I guess I could certainly spare some for you." So Penny enjoyed her first meal in her new home with her new friend.

While she ate her lunch, her thoughts returned to the beautiful piano in the parlor. She thought about her grandmother and how she loved to play.

"I know," she suddenly exclaimed. The dog raised his head, looking at her expectantly "I'll call you Wanger Doops! " When her grandmother was a little girl, she had a dog whose name was Wanger Doops. She had named him after a song that was popular at the time, *The Wang-Wang Blues*." She recalled her grandmother's stories about her dog howling something terrible whenever she would sing the words to the song. Penny's grandmother had been on her mind a lot the last few days, so it only seemed natural. "What do you think of that for a name?"

The dog raised his head and looked at her, raising one eyebrow "Yes, I think that is a good name for you. Wanger Doops it is."

"Here Wanger Doops," she called. But he didn't budge.

"That is kind of a mouthful. Maybe I could shorten it. How about Wang?"

He gave a short yip. Penny believed that his response showed that he approved of the name. "Wang it is then."

"Bet you're not going to like this, but I think we need to get you in to see a vet. Bet you haven't had any shots. And you really need a bath."

Penny took her phone and looked up local veterinarians. Finding one in downtown Gannon Ridge, she gave them a call and made an appointment to take Wang in to see him.

The rest of the day Penny spent cleaning the apartment in the back of the big house. Uncle Harry had lived in that apartment and now she thought it would also be perfect for her. After the initial cleaning was done, she felt that she could move into it right away. There was a kitchenette in the apartment so she would not have to wait until the big kitchen was done to move in.

From what Penny had seen of Burr Oak, she was delighted. It was everything she had hoped for and more. Her dream had been of a big old house, which she could open and make into a Bed & Breakfast and this was absolutely perfect. The five rooms upstairs were made to order for guestrooms. The large dining area, the huge kitchen, and the enormous parlor had her just trembling with excitement.

The big carriage house could be made into a tea and gift shop, which was another dream of Penny's. The upstairs living quarters could be rented out. Hopefully, it could be rented to someone she could hire to work with the Bed & Breakfast and/or shop. Her dream for the shop was to grow and sell herbs. She even had a name in mind for it; *The Tea Cozy*. Penny loved herbs and she had grown several in large containers on the roomy ledge outside her apartment window in the city. She grew as many as she could, drying them and cooking with both fresh and dried throughout the year. Penny was not much of a coffee drinker, but she did like her cup of tea. And her own herbal tea blend was a special treat for her.

Other plans for the shop were rattling around in Penny's head as well. She thought she might be able to sell her own tea blends. She wanted to have a tea bar (rather than a coffee bar.) A daily pastry or scone would go well with the tea. Maybe some of that delicious kettle corn that Linda Booth made. *I will have to schedule a meeting with her after I get moved in.* And, of course, a space for kids, too. Books to read, games to play while their parents shopped. But the big house was top on the list for now.

The next order of business was to go back into town and enlist the help that would be needed to renovate the big house and begin to bring the plans for the B & B to fruition. The Inn would be a good place to start asking questions.

# Chapter Four

As Penny drove back into town, she looked around at the scenic beauty of the river valley. This side of the river was dotted with limestone bluffs, rising high above the river. She could just imagine how beautiful the trees on those bluffs would look later in the fall. It would provide a gorgeous view from Burr Oak.

The river road produced a lot of traffic with weekenders using the auto tour routes to spend time with their families, camping, boating and other recreational activities. With the Gannon Ridge Inn being the only overnight establishment in the town, Penny believed that a Bed & Breakfast could still do a thriving business and not take away from Joe's business, or Meg's either for that matter.

Gannon Ridge boasted several different attractions, which brought people into town. There was The Pottery Shack, which consisted of a sales room in front and a workshop in back. The art museum, several antique shops, a movie theater, bowling alley, and even several good trout streams nearby which enticed fishermen (and their families) from miles around. Gannon Hill College on the outskirts of town was a small, private 4-year college. The big attraction, of course, was the Col. Tom steamship that provided cruises up and down the river. Gannon Ridge was a busy town for its size.

Meg's Diner was doing a brisk business when Penny arrived, as it was time for the evening meal. But that didn't prevent Meg from spying her right away "Hi, there, Penny. How did the cleaning job go?"

"It's a big job, but I am so excited about doing it. I have the apartment in the back cleaned and I am so anxious to move in there. Which is something I want to talk to you about."

Meg look startled and said he'd come and visit with her as soon as he brought her order. So Penny ordered and sat back to look at the customers in Meg's. There were couples, families, and single diners. Meg's appealed to all.

"Well, what is it you wanted to talk about? What's this about you moving in there?" asked Meg as he set Penny's order on the table before her.

"I want to open a Bed & Breakfast at Burr Oak. In the meantime, I am going to move into the apartment in the back. That is now my new residence." Penny had decided she might as well spit it right out No use dilly dallying about. But Meg's reaction truly surprised her.

"Humph!"

"Why do you say that?"

"Because that's a big undertaking. Cost a lot. May not be worth it. People won't come there to stay. No reason to."

Well, that certainly wasn't what Penny had expected to hear. In fact, that was the last type of response she had expected from him. He had seemed so friendly and forthcoming earlier.

"But you didn't seem to think that when you told me about the house. You even said it would be a big undertaking to fix it up but it would be worth it. And I agree with you. It's built well and mostly needs cleaning."

"Didn't know you wanted to keep it for your own self."

"But why else did you think I came out here?" Penny was beginning to get exasperated with Meg. Quite a change in manner.

"I thought you were going to fix it up to sell, and then go back to the city."

*Ah. So that was it.* "You're saying you want me to leave Gannon Ridge?"

Meg shrugged, saying nothing.

"Well, I guess there is nothing more to be said then, is there?" Having finished her meal, Penny rose from the table and said, "I'd like my bill, please."

It had been a tremendous letdown. Penny was hurt. She had felt such a warm welcome when she first came into town. What had happened to change that feeling? Why did Meg's outlook suddenly change once he found out she was staying in Gannon Ridge? It was a puzzle and Penny didn't feel up to puzzles right now.

Penny drove back to the Inn and went in to the office. Joe looked up when she entered.

"Hi, Penny How's it going up there?"

*Take the bull by the horns. Tell him.* "Joe, what would you say if I told you I would like to make a Bed & Breakfast out of Burr Oak and run it myself?"

Joe smiled, "Comes as no surprise to me. What else would you be doing here, a lady alone with such a big house?"

Penny told him of Meg's reaction to her announcement. "He reacted totally different from how you did just now."

Joe shrugged, "I'm not surprised. Meg is kind of new to Gannon Ridge. Only been here a couple of years. He has kind of thought he'd like to buy Burr Oak and open a big restaurant there. Always talking about it, but everyone knew he didn't have the funds to fix it up himself and, of course, it was never put on the market. I suppose he thought you would spend the money to fix it up and then put it on the market. Then he would buy it. Though I don't think he could have gotten funding for that big a venture. He doesn't even own the diner"

Now Penny felt bad for Meg. He had a dream just like she had her dream. She knew how she would feel if her Bed & Breakfast bubble were popped by some newcomer to town. Penny hoped this wouldn't be a setback in her endeavor. After all, these people were her neighbors now and she wanted to be friends with them.

"Joe, I'm going to need to hire some help. First to help with cleaning and getting the house ready to open the Bed & Breakfast. Then later to help with the running of it. Do you have any ideas?"

"Sure do. Stop out at Gannon Hill College and put a notice up on the bulletin board. College kids out there are always looking for work. Summer classes are still in session so there should be a number of students around. Then the fall students will soon be arriving."

"Wonderful idea. Thanks, Joe."

Penny would drive out to the college Monday morning before she went back to work at Burr Oak. She would move into the suite at the big house. Penny didn't plan to set back idle. She could still work while she was thinking things out. Besides, there was Wang there at the big house waiting for her.

Penny stopped at the door. "Hey, Joe. Have you ever seen a big, light brown dog around?"

"Sure. The town stray, I guess you could call him. Nobody seems to know where he hangs out, but he's no bother to anyone. Folks tend to leave him food where he can get it. Why, did you meet up with him?"

"Sure did. We seem to have adopted each other. Wanted to make sure he didn't belong to anyone before I got too attached to him."

"Sounds good. I think he must be afraid of people. At least of kids. He won't let them pet him. And the funny thing is, he seems to steer clear of the sheriff and his deputy. It's like he knows they will pick up strays if they find them"

"I think he's a doll. Just like a big old soft teddy bear. His fur looks like velvet"

# Chapter Five

The next morning after checking out of the Inn, Penny went to the grocery store and stocked up on groceries to take to her new home. *Good thing I have the Honda because stocking empty shelves takes up a lot of space.* She also bought a sack of dog food, a couple of dog dishes, a collar, and some chew toys. Penny and her new friend were going to have a good time.

Penny saw a greenhouse on the way out of town and decided to stop and see if they had any herbs. She wanted to get some annuals to plant before it got too late. She did find some basil and sage and bought several plants of each.

On the way to Burr Oak, Penny drove out to Gannon Hill College to put up the help-wanted notice. It was a nice looking campus. The green hills of the campus seemed to beckon to the students she saw there. She hoped that she would fine the perfect people to help her. She located the bulletin board and placed her help-wanted ad on it.

When Penny arrived at Burr Oak, she was disappointed to find that Wang didn't seem to be around. *Maybe I had scared him off. I suppose I might have been in too big a hurry to buy the dog things.*

Penny got the dog items for Wang out of the Honda first and took them into the apartment. Putting water in one dish, she poured some of the food into the other. She took them out the back door and set them on the porch.

Penny had no idea how Wang came into the house. Yeah, now that she thought about it, how did he get in? The doors were all shut and locked. Maybe a window, she thought, so she took a tour of the house to see if there was an open window. While Penny was looking for that opening, she discovered one of the doors upstairs led up to a large attic. *I'll have to take time to explore that later.*

But all the windows were closed tightly; no place where a 4-pawed critter could have gotten in. She was stumped. Unless...of course, that was it! He had gotten into the house after she was already there the day before. *I must have left the door open. Sure glad that's cleared up.*

Penny began unloading the groceries and stocking the cupboard shelves and the refrigerator that she had cleaned the day before. When the Honda was unloaded, she started cleaning the parlor. It was a big room. She took off the tarps that covered the rolled-up area rugs from both the parlor and dining room and hauled them outside and hung them on the veranda rail. Maybe they just needed to be aired out, at least for now. Later she would check into getting them cleaned. Then she cleaned the beautiful hard wood floors.

The grand piano was interesting and she found herself being drawn once again to it. No telling how old it was. After dusting the insides, Penny sat down and began playing the first thing that came to mind, "Beyond the Sunset". That was her grandmother's favorite song.

*This one is for you, Grandma.*

There were some flat notes there somewhere and the chords didn't sound right. She knew it would take some work to perfect the sound again. The three years of cold winters and hot summers had been hard on it. Hopefully there was someone nearby who repaired and tuned pianos.

The parlor had two sets of French doors. Each had ornate glass door knobs. One set led to the west veranda and the other set opened into the entryway. Once the glass was cleaned and a little Old English applied to the wood, the doors looked beautiful.

Penny had spent the entire morning working in the parlor and was getting hungry, so she went to her apartment and fixed herself a ham and cheese sandwich. She meant to set down at her table to eat it, but was still too buoyed up to settle. So taking her sandwich, she had a walking lunch while looking over the work she had done and what needed to be done yet.

*I wonder why this house was built so huge,* Penny thought. And what on earth had Uncle Harry done with such a big house. He had never said anything about why he lived in such a big house. She had never seen any family pictures. He had been married, but Uncle Harry said his wife and son had died although she didn't know how long ago that had been. He never talked anymore about them. Penny could see it was hard on him to talk about them so she never asked again.

*Well, time to get back to work.* This time she wanted to clean the library. She wanted to set up her desk top computer in there once it was clean and the hook-ups were in. As she opened the door to the library, Penny was startled at first to see Wang lying there on the rug.

"Wang! I'm so glad you came back. Did you see the food I put out by the back door for you? Come here, boy I want to show you what I got for you today."

Wang eagerly followed her back to her apartment, tail wagging. She opened the back door and looked at the dog dishes, but they didn't appear to have been touched. Picking them up, Penny brought them inside the door. She would make it a point to feed him there from now on. After Wang had eaten, Penny gave him the chew toy and he settled down happily on the rug.

Leaving Wang to enjoy his new toy, Penny took the cleaning supplies into the library. However, Wang followed her bringing his new chew toy with him. Guess he didn't like being alone in this big empty house either. That was fine by her, as she enjoyed his company.

There were several good-sized boxes in the library full of books. The books were stored in plastic inside the boxes. They were a little musty smelling but nothing a little fresh air couldn't cure. There was floor to ceiling bookshelves on two walls of the library. It would have been quite an expense to fill those shelves with books. She was glad the books were still here.

Penny pulled a chair up and sat down to go through the books in one of the boxes. There were some treasures in this box. She was thrilled that some were real classics. As she continued to go through the boxes of books, Penny found even more treasures. Some books had no doubt been on the library's shelves back when Thomas Gannon had occupied the house. They were veritable museum pieces. There were also several journals belonging to Thomas Gannon. How nice for Bed & Breakfast patrons to be able to use this library.

Next came the cleaning of the shelves so that she would be able to put the books on a clean area once she had opened the rest of the boxes.

Penny was just finishing the last shelf when she heard the sound of a vehicle in front of the house. Leaving the library, she made her way out to the front entryway

Wang suddenly rose and barked. Penny went to the door and discovered that the telephone man had arrived. He really didn't seem too surprised at the number of things she wanted him to do. Being a local he knew about Burr Oak and even about Penny. He knew it was a big house and that she would need several phones. By now word had spread that Penny was going to open a Bed & Breakfast.

There were only two phone jacks in the whole house, one in her apartment and one in the parlor. Penny had him install a phone in the upstairs hallway for the guests to use, one in the dining room, and one in the kitchen. He installed both the phone jack and another line for a computer in her apartment, and an extra computer line for customers to come into the library and hook up their laptops along with a phone line. It was after 5:00 and the phone man needed to leave, but said that he would be back in the morning to finish. Penny would call the Internet company to set up her service. And the cable company. She would wait on the phone lines to the carriage house. She still had a lot of renovation to do there.

Another busy day and now Penny could get ready to settle in. She was tired and decided not to do anymore work today or she would be too tired, not to mention a little sore. Penny went to her apartment and fixed dinner. Since it was a beautiful evening, she decided to take her meal out on the west veranda to eat. She took some reading materials and spent the rest of the evening there. Wang came too and lay near her chair.

"Wang, what do you think about this place? Isn't it a beautiful house? It's sure taking a lot of work to do everything I want to do. But I'm glad I came here. And I'm glad you're here too." Penny scratched his left ear and hugged him. As the sun dipped down in the western sky, Penny scratched Wang behind his left ear again and said "Well, Wang, I'm tired and ready to fall into bed. Want to come?"

Wang eagerly followed her as she locked the front door and went back to her apartment. Penny left the door to the apartment open. She figured that Wang might need to explore during the night.

# Chapter Six

As the sun rose the next morning, Penny saw that it was the dawn of a beautiful day. It was so bright that the light came through the windows into her bedroom. Penny stretched and yawned. But as she tried to move, she found that she could not move her legs. She panicked, thinking about her father's debilitating stroke. As she became more awake, she realized that Wang was lying across her legs.

*Silly goose*, she thought silently admonishing herself. Penny got up and let Wang outside, then went to shower.

Penny had just finished cleaning up after breakfast when the phone rang - her cell phone. She didn't have the main system yet. Upon answering it she heard a young female voice on the other end. Her name was Elizabeth Colton and she was inquiring as to the ad that Penny had left at the college.

"I found your ad on the bulletin board and I and some of my friends would be interested in talking to you about what positions would need to be filled. If today would be good for you, the four of us don't have classes this afternoon and we would like to visit with you then, if that would be agreeable to your schedule."

Overjoyed that she had received a response to her ad so soon, not to mention that she might possibly get all the positions filled at the same time, Penny agreed upon 2:00 and hung up.

"Well Wang, we are going to have company this afternoon. Four college students are coming by to see about the positions I advertised for. We'll have to get something ready for a little bite to eat. Young people are always hungry."

Penny looked at her watch. It was time to head into town for Wang's appointment. "Wang, want to go for a ride in my Honda?" She didn't know if he would fight it or not. Hence the ruse of a car ride.

Wang seemed to enjoy setting in the passenger seat up front with Penny. She was thrilled that he seemed to want to be with her. She had wanted a dog for as long as she could remember. It just wasn't feasible until now.

Soon they pulled up in front of a building. The sign said it was the Gannon Ridge Pet Clinic. Penny shut off the engine and retrieving the leash she had purchased from the back seat, she fastened it to Wang's collar. He sat perfectly still. So far, so good, thought Penny.

Penny opened the door and let Wang out. They walked up to the front door, opened it and walked in. He was so good, Penny was amazed. The receptionist took her information and said that Dr. Warren would be with them shortly.

The rest of the appointment went just as smoothly. Even Dr. Warren was surprised. Wang was given his shots. Next an assistant took him to another room and gave him a trim and a bath. When she brought the new and improved Wang back to Penny, she was pleased with how nice he looked. She gave him a hug, burying her nose in his fur.

"Wang, my man. You look divine and you smell so good."

Dr. Warren told Penny that he thought Wang was mostly a yellow lab. "He's in good health and we now have him up-to-date on his shots."

Returning to Burr Oak, Penny decided that it was time to call back east and have the moving van come with the rest of her things. Penny put in the call and found that they could leave the end of next week. Hopefully, she would have help then to put things where she wanted. The bedrooms should be cleaned and painted by then. Penny was excited about having everything arrive.

Having furnishings for three bedrooms, Penny was anxious to put them into the bedrooms. That would mean she only had to get furnishings for three more bedrooms, as one was for her apartment. And she also had some personal things that she would like to have in her apartment. There was a writing desk that had belonged to her grandmother. Having some of her own things that had become a comfort for her would be nice.

Soon 2:00 rolled around and Penny heard the sound of an automobile at the same time that Wang excitedly began barking. The two of them went to the front door and greeted their guests.

Elizabeth Colton seemed to be a take-charge kind of girl or maybe it was just because she had been the one who called "Hello, I'm Elizabeth Colton but everyone calls me Bitsy. It started out to be Betsy but it just gravitated to Bitsy because of my size. I don't mind at all. I'm the one who spoke to you on the phone. These are my friends, Paul Engelhard, Jackie Everett and her brother, Jason."

Penny shook their hands as they were introduced. You could certainly tell that Jackie and Jason were brother and sister. They looked enough alike to be twins "Won't you come in? Let's go back to my apartment where we can be comfortable."

As the young people found seats and made themselves comfortable, Penny got out the little sandwiches and bars that she had prepared and some sodas. The young men ate as though they had missed lunch.

Jackie and her brother Jason were both blond with the same wavy hair and both had blue eyes. They were both tall. Paul was also tall, but with black hair. Bitsy had reddish hair and freckles. Penny mentioned that Jackie and Jason looked like twins.

"That's what everybody says. We are twins!" Jackie gave her brother's arm a squeeze and he smiled fondly at her. *That's nice*, Penny thought. All four of them seemed to be quite fond of each other.

Penny explained what type of work would need to be done. Some specialized skills were required but at first it would be a lot of grunt work. She also explained about wanting to open the Bed & Breakfast, which they already knew about (small town again.) There would be advertising to be done, decorating, and an entertainment program just to name a few. Then Penny gave them details about the shop she wanted in the carriage house. They toured the house and the carriage house.

When they returned to the apartment they got down to business about what they could do. They seemed about as excited as she had been. Even Wang seemed to want to be a part of it all. He kept close by, even nuzzling in close to Penny on the sofa while they talked.

Paul's major was computer programming and he said that could be useful in developing a web site for both the Bed & Breakfast and the shop.

He would also be able to set up a software program for guest reservations and billing.

Jackie was an art major. While they had been talking, her pencil had been flying over her sketchpad. She turned it around for Penny to see. The drawing was of Penny with Wang nestled against her. This was fantastic! There could be big possibilities with that talent. Penny was giddy with the thought of it all. Jackie said that she enjoyed doing caricatures. Perhaps she could do them for the guests for a small fee.

Jason's major was music. He planned to go into teaching music. It was no wonder his eyes lit up when he saw the grand piano in the parlor.

Bitsy's major was Marketing and Public Relations. She would be an asset to the advertising side of the Bed & Breakfast Jackie's art and Paul's computer knowledge would also be a winning combination. Penny could see big possibilities with Jason's music too, especially with that grand piano in the parlor.

"I really impressed with all of your skills. I'm willing to offer you the positions and give you all the hours you can use. Since you will be using the skills you have for your majors I'll also be happy to give recommendations after graduations or to help towards any credits."

Penny told them that next week the moving van was coming so they would have to have the bedrooms cleaned and painted to make room for those things. As the afternoon wore on, they made plans to begin the next day. Penny realized that not all four would always be able to come at the same time and that classes would sometimes prevent a lot of work getting done. But they promised her they all four would all be available at 10:00 the next day.

After they left Penny asked Wang "Well, what did you think? Am I making a good decision to hire them?"

Wang's happy yip seemed to seal the matter.

Later while Wang and Penny were working upstairs in one of the bedrooms, they heard a voice coming from downstairs in the entryway "Yoo whooo! Anybody home?"

Wang took off for the stairs, emitting woofs as he sped towards the sound of the voice. Penny hurried after him. She hadn't learned his ways yet to know if he would tear into a visitor or just great them.

The lady at the door was middle-aged with red hair that looked like it had a life of its own. Her friendly, smiling face sported lots of freckles. When Penny reached the entryway, the visitor was stroking Wang and talking to him. Wang, great watchdog that he is, was soaking it all in.

"Hello, I'm Penny Powers. What can I do for you?" Penny said reaching out to shake hands with the red-head.

She straightened up and shook Penny's hand.

"Land sakes alive there, missy! I'm Dotty Emerson I apologize for barging in on you this way. But with you having no phone listing yet, well."

"Let's go back to my apartment," Penny said. "I'm ready for a little break anyway. How about a glass of iced herbal tea?"

"Well, golly scissors! Don't mind if I do," responded the vocally colorful Dotty.

As they made themselves comfortable seated with a glass of herbal ice tea each,

Dotty explained her reason for coming.

"First I wanted to welcome you to Gannon Ridge. Saints preserve us but it sure is good to have someone in Burr Oak again. It's been a coon's age since someone lived in the big house. The town grapevine has it that you are planning to open a Bed & Breakfast. And that comes to my second reason for coming. Ed, he's my better half, said that maybe I could talk to you about taking me on as cook since I love to do that. And good at it, if I do say so myself. So, quick as a wink, I hightailed it up here."

"Yes, I will need someone in that capacity. What are your qualifications for such a position? Do you have any experience?"

"I used to have my own catering business. I was happy as a clam doing it too, but we fell on some hard times and had to sell the van and the equipment to pay for bills. Ed was injured in an accident a couple of years ago and though we had insurance, well, gee whiz …, you know……."

"I brought my folder ……..with pictures of my specialties along with the recipes," Dotty continued. "Most are my own recipes……. change 'em to go with what's available. Only use the recipes to make a note of ingredients needed. "

Penny hadn't been long into the conversation with Dotty before she realized that Dotty hardly ever finished a sentence. And that she also had quite a unique way of turning a phrase. And she nearly felt breathless herself just listening to Dotty talk. She and Dotty should get along fine.

"This is wonderful, Dotty. I think you are just the person I need. But the position you will be taking will be as Burr Oak's chef, not cook. Burr Oak will be a high end Bed and Breakfast. Welcome aboard."

# Chapter Seven

Morning dawned once again and another day of work began at Burr Oak. During Penny's visits with Dotty and the four college students, they had agreed to a team meeting periodically. It would be good to pool resources and skills and come up with a game plan. Actually, several game plans. They just needed to be sorted through to decide which should be done first. Brainstorming, that's what was needed, just like she used to do in her father's business. A team meeting would help to achieve that.

It was following one of those team meetings that Penny decided to get out for a breath of fresh air "Come on, Wang," called Penny. "Let's go for a walk." Wang rushed eagerly to her side, anticipating a romp in the woods with his favorite person. As they walked down an old path back of the carriage house, Penny kept a running conversation going with Wang.

"I suppose this path has been here since Col. Gannon and his family first settled here," she mused. "Maybe even a lot of different dogs have walked alongside their owners too."

Wang paused and looked up at Penny, then turned and she continued. "I wonder what goes on in that head of yours." Wang merely continued walking.

"You know something, Wang? Fixing up this house is going to be a joy for me. Already I love this town and the people in it. The hustle and bustle of the big city is not present here. It's so peaceful. Uncle Harry was right about this town. It's one of a kind."

Penny reached up to twist a dead twig from a low-hanging branch. "Okay, Wang time for some fun!" Penny tossed the twig ahead of them and Wang eagerly raced off to retrieve it and bring it back to her. They played this way for a while as they continued on down the path. Suddenly the path ended high above the Mississippi River. The ledge had once had and ornate iron fence protecting anyone from straying too close to the precipice. Most of the fence was still there.

"This was a beautiful fence at one time," she said to Wang "I wonder if we can repair it to its original condition. I think this path can be maintained without too much trouble for our guests to enjoy. It's a pleasant surprise to come upon this scene. I'm sure my guests will enjoy it."

Another path went away from the ledge in the opposite direction. It appeared to head toward town. "We'll save that for next time," Penny promised. "Time to go back to the house. Come on, Wang."

The paths were overgrown and strewn with dead branches and leaves. It would be good to fix up the paths for the Bed & Breakfast guests to walk or bike. The one going into town would be handy for the guests who might want to walk or bike into town.

Penny decided that now with her crew busy working on the B & B, that she would give Linda Booth a call and invite her over for coffee, or tea.

Penny waited while the phone rang several times. She was about to hang up when a breathless Linda answered. "Booths, Linda speaking."

"Oh hi, Linda. I hope you weren't busy. This is Penny Powers."

"Hi, Penny. Yes, would you believe I couldn't find that blamed phone? Glad you didn't give up on me."

"You said I should give you a call and we could meet for coffee. Or do you like iced tea?"

"Iced tea sounds wonderful in this heat."

"Great. How would tomorrow be here at Burr Oak, say about 2:00?"

"Sounds, great, Penny. See you then."

# Chapter Eight

The next day, Linda Booth was right on time. Penny greeted her at the main door.

"Hi, Linda. So glad you could come. Come on in."

"Thanks. Nice of you to ask me. Wow, the place looks terrific."

"Would you like a tour before we go back to my apartment for refreshments?"

"I sure would. I hear you are going to open a B & B."

Penny smiled. "Word sure does get around. Maybe I won't even have to advertise."

"I know," said Linda." Gannon Ridge is just like one big family."

"Let's start here in this room," Penny said, leading her guest into the parlor.

As Penny revealed the remaining rooms and the plans she had for them, Linda commented that she thought it must be exciting to do all this and all by herself.

"Well, I'm not really by myself. I have hired four students from the college to help out. I also have Dotty Emerson, who is my chef."

"My, you really do have things under control. Dotty will be wonderful in the position of chef"

"I have had business experience in New York," and Penny told her of the story of how she came to be in Gannon Ridge.

"The only business I have experience in is the Kettle Corn booth. Jerry and I bought the equipment a couple of years ago. We just have a booth at things like local county fairs and town celebrations like Col. Tom Days. Maybe someday we can grow enough to call it a full time business for both of us."

"That's interesting, Linda. Because I have a proposition for you."

"I'm all ears."

Penny laid out for Linda her plans for the Tea Cozy and her desire to carry Booth's Kettle Corn in the shop.

"We won't be opening it right away. I want to get the B & B opened up and then there will be a lot of remodeling to do before *The Tea Cozy* would be ready for business. But I hope to have it going by late fall," Penny explained. "What do you think? Are you interested?"

Linda was over-joyed. "What a wonderful opportunity. I'm all for it. Of course, I will have to discuss it first with Jerry. But I'm sure he will be as excited about it as I am."

"Okay then. Let's have some iced tea and cookies."

# Chapter Nine

Over the next few weeks, many changes came about at Burr Oak and much work was accomplished. The team from Gannon Hill, Dotty, and Penny had a good working camaraderie, which allowed them to complete many of the tasks on their list. Penny grew very fond of her staff. In time she came to think of them as her family.

There came a time when the bedrooms were painted and wallpapered. The bedroom furniture, which had been ordered, had arrived and the rooms had been completely furnished. Penny's belongings had arrived from the city. The rooms were now ready for occupation. The walking path had been groomed and the fence rail overlooking the river had been repaired. The Bed & Breakfast guests would now be able to hike or bike to town and back if they desired.

One day when everyone was busy with their various jobs, Bisty and Jackie came running into the kitchen trembling with excitement. Bitsy caught her breath and said, "Penny, have you been up to the attic?"

"Why, no I haven't," Penny said "I just got too busy and completely forgot about it. Why?"

"Well, you've got to come up there now and see what we found. Come on, everybody. Drop what you are doing and come along."

So up to the attic the troop went, wondering what on earth could be so exciting in a dusty old attic. But when Penny saw what had caused the girls to be so keyed up, she found good reason for their exuberance. The place was full of fine old period furniture. There were several steamer trunks, and on closer scrutiny, they discovered they were full of old clothes – really old clothes! There were lots more boxes of books and boxes of papers.

"Penny, did you see this big old dining table? It's so big I don't know how they got it up here," Jackie fairly squealed with joy "I think its oak, which would make sense, given all the oak trees outside."

"That would be great to use in the dining room. And look, there are several leaves for it. All we need are chairs to go with it," Penny said. But she looked around and didn't see any chairs.

"You can always order chairs to match the style," interposed Paul. This is a great old table. It would be worth using if you really want to keep things from the period"

"Well, it's settled then. We'll use this table if you guys can figure out how to get it down." It took some doing but before long Paul and Jason had the table relocated to the dining room.

The dining hall was easy. New paint, wallpaper, and drapes had been added. The huge oak table was in great shape, so they decided to keep it. New chairs were ordered to match the table as closely as possible.

The parlor had been Penny's joy to refurbish. In all their work in the house, they had tried to keep the walls and furnishings as authentic as the original as possible. However, Penny did take certain license with the parlor. She had an elaborate entertainment center installed with a large-screen TV, stereo, and DVD player. The piano had been restored and tuned, although at quite a cost. Even then it wasn't perfect but it would do. The beauty of the piece made up for the sound quality. Two small tables were set up at one end for playing games. A number of games were in the game cabinet. The fireplace was fully functional having been thoroughly cleaned. A brand new Foosball table stood at the other end of the parlor. The younger guests would enjoy that.

In the library, a wide selection of books that would amaze avid readers had been arranged on the shelves. There was even a shelf devoted to children in case guests would be bringing their children. The computer had been installed for guests to use. The fireplace in the library was pronounced unusable by the chimney sweep. He said it was a fake. Imagine that. Oh well, at least they had one in all the other rooms, and Penny had one of her own in her apartment. At least some of the ambiance would be present just by seeing the authentic-looking fireplace. Penny did wonder though, why it was not real. It seemed that a house that had been heated in this fashion with a fireplace in every room would need a real one in the library. *Perhaps that had been the case originally, but had been changed as more modern heating methods emerged.*

Bitsy had been working on a press release to announce the opening of the new Bed & Breakfast. Jennifer had developed the artwork that went into the brochures and Paul established a web site for the business. Jackie also helped Dotty with the artwork on the menus. Paul set up the business software on Penny's computer. Penny was overjoyed at how the young people worked together. Even Dotty had become an important part of their little family. And let's don't forget Wanger Doops! As Dotty would say, "Heavens to Betsy, but he is a friendly dog and a joy to have around!"

Wang had early seemed to enjoy being with Penny only. But as time went by and he was around the B & B crew, he seemed to consider them party of the family. The college kids loved him and he got along great with them.

Jason had seen to the piano and having it tuned, he made sure there was a good supply of sheet music available. Of course, there had already been some in the piano bench, but he had ordered more. One day a package came for him and his excitement was catching. He called everyone into the parlor while he sat down to play it.

"Remember you said that you named your dog, Wanger Doops, because of the song your grandmother used to sing when she was a girl? Well, I ordered the sheet music for it. Just didn't seem right not to have his special song with the others."

The little group gathered around the piano to read the words while he played the tune. Blues wasn't exactly in Penny's collection of most listened to music but she had enjoyed listening to Jason playing the piano. They gathered round the piano in anticipation. Jason began to play and the little group tried to follow along by singing the strange words.

The Wang-Wang Blues *

Wang, Wang Blues
She's gone and left me with the Wang, Wang Blues;
And let me tell you, mister,
I never knew I'd be so blue until she went away.

Wang, Wang Blues

Wang, Wang Blues
I've got the everlasting Wang, Wang Blues
I'm only asking that my
Sweet will come back and chase those
Wang, Wang Blues

* Words & Music by Gus Muller, Buster Johnson & Henry
   (Words obtained on the Internet)

When he had finished playing, they laughed and applauded. Well, the words were a bit strange sounding, and Penny could sure understand why her grandmother's dog would howl! As it was, her own Wang seemed oblivious to what was going on. He had lain down in front of the fireplace with his paws on top of his head. Could he have been holding his ears? Certainly looked like it.

Dotty had done a tremendous job in the kitchen. She had discovered many of the things she would need for running a Bed & Breakfast kitchen boxed up in the large pantry. She reacted like a child at Christmas time as she opened box after box with Penny. The extensive set of antique china with the letter "G" would be great to use. The kitchen was freshly painted and Dotty pronounced it, and her, ready for business.

The chairs for the dining room had not yet arrived, as they had to be specially made. Otherwise, the dining hall was ready for business, too.

They were ready. The opening date had been set for the weekend after Labor Day. Bitsy and Paul had worked hard on getting the information out there so that the public would have an overwhelming desire to come and stay at Burr Oak, Gannon Ridge's authentic new Bed & Breakfast. They were ready for business - well, almost. The chairs for the dining table had still not arrived. Penny was beginning to fret about that matter. She could just see people standing at the dining table instead of setting. Dotty said not to worry. "We can always have it buffet-style and the guests can come to the parlor to be seated."

"That's a great idea and I could play classic tunes on the piano while they gather in the parlor," said Jason.

"Most people will probably stand or walk around anyway," added Jackie.

Penny had to smile to herself. Jason really loves that piano, she thought. She was so glad that they were able to restore it. It had been spendy, but worth the cost and Jason could really make the piano come alive when he played. It was enjoyable to listen to him play, to watch his face as he immersed himself into the music.

The five guestrooms were ready to go. Three couples had sent in reservations for the first open house weekend. That left two openings yet. Not bad for a business that isn't even open yet.

One evening, Penny was in the library late, seated at the big desk and working on the computer. It was after midnight. She wanted to get the confirmation emails sent to those three couples before they had a chance to change their minds. She had been working there so long that the only light in the house was in the library. Wang was curled up in his favorite place on the rug in front of the fireplace. The house was still - not a sound.

Suddenly, Wang stood up; his ears cocked. A quiet rumble started in his throat. So quiet that you would have had to be quite close to him to hear it. He stood ever so still, looking in one direction only.

The rumbling in Wang's throat ceased, but still he looked at the fireplace. Then reason entered Penny's head again. *Of course, it was only mice. After all, this was an old house. It stands to reason there would be some mice in the walls.*

"Wang, it's okay, boy. It's only mice. We sure are scarredy cats tonight. Guess we better call it a night."

Penny switched off the computer and Wang followed her out of the library to her quarters with one last look at the fireplace as he left. "I will have to talk to the boys tomorrow about taking care of those.

# Chapter Ten

The day for the open house was nearing. Bitsy had been very busy sending out press releases, and with Jackie's artistic talents, had put out posters, fliers etc. With Jason helping by making a web page for the Bed & Breakfast, the information regarding the open house was also getting out.

Dotty had been holed up in the kitchen planning for the food end of the open house. As the day drew nearer, she hardly seemed to leave there at all until it was time to go home for the day  "Got too much work… Busy as a bee," she would say.

Dotty had even convinced her husband Ed to construct a wooden sign for Burr Oak Bed & Breakfast -- out of oak, of course. The carving on the sign was superb workmanship. This gave Penny a wonderful idea. Ed had been laid off from his construction job and seemed to be at loose ends. Dotty had recently confided in Penny that they would probably have to move from their home into something more affordable.

Penny talked to Dotty about her idea as she was working on the final touches the day before the open house. "Dotty," she said "You know that I plan to work on the carriage house and turn it into a shop, don't you?"

"Yes, Penny I knew that. It's…well…it's a super duper idea"

"Well, I also want to work on the apartment above it. I have an idea about how I can get that work done and how you can solve some of your problems all with the same solution."

"Yes, go on," she said "I'm all ears….."

"Since Ed is without a position at the present time and you will soon have to move, I was wondering if you would be willing to move into the carriage house apartment and Ed could work on both it and the shop. He could do the work in place of the rent for a while. What do you think?"

Dotty was ecstatic. "Oh, Penny! That would be...... Well, I think it just, ...it's so...Well, golly scissors! Wait till I tell Ed! I'm almost sure he will say okay! Penny, you're just as sweet as honey to do this. I just don't know how to thank you......Jeepers creepers! This is great!" She gave Penny a bear hug.

"Okay, well, you talk to Ed tonight and see what he says. Of course, the apartment will need a little work done before you can move in. It's mainly cleaning though. Some things could be worked on after you are in there. I would want you to get that finished before we start working on the shop. We've got enough for a while to keep us busy with the B & B."

Dotty was ready to go for the night and would be back early in the morning to finish the things that could not be done a day ahead. Dotty had the desserts ready for the open house tomorrow. The open house was to begin at 1:00. Excitement was mounting. They were all rushing around fixing last minute things. The kids were as excited as she was. In fact, her little team of workers had taken a personal attitude about the whole establishment. It belonged to them all. As Dotty so aptly put it, "everybody's running around like chickens with their heads cut off!"

Penny closed and locked the doors for the night. She and Wang headed into her apartment. But he didn't stay long. Usually he would come into her bedroom when she retired for the night. But tonight he didn't seem to want to come in with her.

"Okay. Suit yourself," Penny chided him "You do what ever you want to do." She was tired and didn't feel like coaxing him to come with her. So leaving the door open to her apartment, Penny headed for bed and the blissful sleep of the weary.

The day of the open house at the Bed & Breakfast arrived with a splash. A splash of sunshine, that is. Answers to their prayers for a beautiful day for the open house were abounding. The sunrise was beautiful. The weather was warm. There was a soft, gentle breeze, and best of all, Penny's staff was as excited as she was. They had all worked so heard to bring this special day about. This was their day as much as it was hers. She was very proud of the work they had put into it.

Penny and her staff met in the kitchen to go over any last minute preparations. The girls had gone over the furniture, obliterating any dust that may have settled overnight. Dotty enlisted the help of the young men to bring the trays out of the walk-in refrigerator. They all wheeled the carts to the dining room that held the dishes and silverware. They had opted to use the china with the "G" on it rather than paper plates. They would have to wash dishes to keep up with the flow of guests, but Penny really wanted to use that old china. Dotty pronounced everything "fit and shiny as a new dime."

"Has anyone seen Wang yet today?" asked Jason. "I thought I'd corral him before guests began arriving, but there's no sign of him."

"Well, that is strange. I don't remember seeing him this morning when I got up," Penny said thoughtfully. "Usually he's underfoot following us all around." She didn't mention that he refused to sleep in her room last night. "I'll check his dish and see if he has been there."

A quick check of Wang's food and water dishes revealed that he had not yet eaten this morning. "Wang, here Wang, come here boy," she called. But there was no response.

Penny left her apartment and walked down the hallway, continuing to call his name.

A noise. *Where did that come from?* Penny held her breath. *Yes, there it is again, coming from the library. Scratching at the door, and whining. Has to be Wang.*

Penny opened the door and there he stood, his tail waging with great anticipation "Ah ha. Got yourself shut in here and couldn't get out to eat, is it?"

Penny stood to one side and held the door open for him to go through. But he didn't come; he merely looked at her strangely. Can dogs look condescendingly? "Don't you want out so you can go eat?" Penny asked.

Instead of leaving the library, he turned and walked over to the fireplace. It was then that Penny noticed the gaping hole where the fireplace had been. She stood looking at it, transfixed "How did this happen?" She asked of no one in particular.

Wang put his front paws up against a protruding book and pushed it back in place. With a lot of creaking and grinding noises, the fireplace swung back into place.

Penny's attention returned to Wang. She was dumbfounded.

"Wanger Doops! You amaze me. How on earth did you ever do that?"

Wang put his paw on a button on the shelf and pushed. The fireplace once again disappeared and the book protruded again. A secret passageway. By this time it became evident to Penny that Wang wanted to show her something in that passageway.

"Wang, I don't have time to go exploring today. I've got work to do to get ready for the open house."

Wang barked and ran back and forth between Penny and the fireplace. He continued to bark.

"What's going on in here," asked Jason as he and his friends, along with Dotty, entered the library.

Penny merely pointed silently to the opening in the fireplace "For the love of Mike; what...." exclaimed Dotty upon observing the opened fireplace.

"How did that happen?" Betsy asked.

"Wang opened a secret passageway," said Penny. As Wang became even more excited, Penny explained, "I think he wants me to go exploring, but I don't have time now."

Jason stepped into the passageway. When he re-entered the room, he said, "I think we should go with him. There's something peculiar about the passageway - no cobwebs."

They all stared at him numbly. "So...? What are you saying, Jason?" Bitsy wanted to know.

"I'm saying that Wang would have knocked the cobwebs down at his height. There should be cobwebs higher up, but there isn't any at all. Something taller than a dog has been through the passageway."

"Oh, my," said Dotty fearfully.

"How can you be so sure?" Penny asked.

"That's why I think we should follow Wang. See how frantic he is? He knows something and he wants us to know it too."

"Okay," Penny said. "I'm beginning to think there is more to Wang than meets the eye. Okay, I'll go with him. Jason, why don't you come with me? But the rest of you better finish preparations for the open house. She was thinking about safety in numbers and she didn't really want to go in there by herself.

"Yeah," Jason said "I need a flashlight. Be right back."

"Bring one for me, too," Penny called to his disappearing back.

Dotty shuddered as she looked into the passageway "You wouldn't catch me going in there……..Jeepers creepers! I wouldn't touch that tunnel with a ten foot pole." She turned to leave "I'd better get busy in the kitchen. Somebody's got to do some work around here…….."

Bitsy, Jackie and Paul followed her out of the library as she began issuing instructions. Soon Jason returned with two flashlights. He handed Penny one and said, "Okay, Wang. Lead the way."

"This is unbelievable," Penny said, barely above a whisper. "Why do you suppose they had a hidden passageway like this?"

"Hard to tell," Jason answered quietly. "Might have had something to do with the underground railway for slaves. Being on the river like we are, it was probably and ideal location." He added, "Maybe we'd better not talk. Hard telling if someone is in here or not."

Penny nodded, realizing he couldn't see her agreement. She thought about how they were being led in the dark by a dog. *Maybe we should have called the Sheriff instead*, Penny thought. She dispelled that thought quickly at the image of his marked car in front of the Bed & Breakfast just as the open house was getting under way. *I guess this was the best way after all. We certainly couldn't wait – Wang wouldn't let us.*

They had been walking for some time now. Wang pushed on, never slowing, and Jason and Penny followed obediently. As they descended quite a number of stairs the air became cooler. After the first turn, the passageway continued on in the same direction. If they continued on this way, they would run right into the river.

After several minutes of walking along the narrow passageway, Wang's pace seemed to slow. At one point, he stopped and looked back as if to tell them something. He turned and pushed on. Penny began to notice that up ahead, it didn't seem as dark.

*The proverbial light at the end of the tunnel*, Penny thought grimly.

As they neared the lighter area, they began to hear sounds. Soon Penny was able to distinguish them as river sounds – boat sounds, waves splashing. They had indeed run right into the river. As they neared the opening to the river, they walked into a large room – a cave.

Wang led them to one side and at that point, Penny observed several packing crates stored against one wall. Jason put his flashlight down and opened one crate. It was full of packing straw —and paintings. One crate was standing open. A look at the contents revealed that they were items from Burr Oak. Penny had been too busy to notice they were even missing.

There was the painting of Col. Tom Gannon that had been in the hallway. Also several of the books, old and valuable, from the library.

Penny looked at Jason questioningly. "Smugglers," he whispered. He went to the mouth of the cave and looked around outside. "Looks like no one is about," he said taking his cell phone from his pocket. He turned it back on and began dialing. "I'm calling Sheriff Kane," he explained.

"Sheriff, this is Jason Everett. I'm working with Penny Powers at Burr Oak. Her dog just led us down a hidden passageway from the house that opened out into a cave along the river." He paused. "Yeah, I know. But you should see what we found in the cave." He looked at Penny with a grimace and a sign. "Sheriff, I'm serious. I think this is a smuggling site. There are packing crates full of art and other valuables. Some of the contents have been stolen from Burr Oak."

Wang, who had been standing still, suddenly began pacing about. He even whined slightly. That made Penny nervous.

"Sheriff, the dog is becoming agitated. I think you had better send someone in a hurry. They might be coming back. Yes, right below Burr Oak."" Jason flipped his cell phone closed. "Think we…," he started to say, but they both held their breath as they heard the sound of a boat motor. "Quick!" Jason said. "Behind the crates."

Wang followed and the three of them crouched behind the crates as the boat, docked and the motor was killed. *Hopefully, that will be the only thing meeting that sort of end*, was Penny's grim thought.

"Come on boys. Help get some of these crates loaded .We're running behind. I want to get you guys on your way down river so I can go up there to that open house."

Penny's breath caught in her throat. He was planning to go to their open house. This unsavory character, this thief, was going to waltz right into her Burr Oak. The nerve!

"Hey boss, it sure will be a good night for this. When do you think they will be picking the rest of this stuff up?"

The other, evidently the boss, said, "Should be in a day or two, Yancy. Got word from the guys downstream that the pick-up would be soon."

"They sure are a bunch of trusting saps in this hick town. Steal them blind and they don't even know it. What about the rest of the stuff we were going to get from the big house?"

"That has been harder to get to what with that dame moving in and fixing it up. And there's been so many people hanging around, a body can't get in to take anything. Maybe for the next trip. The open house will help. I'm going to go and take a look."

"Mighty nice of them to oblige you and open the place up."

Penny felt Wang tensing beside her. What a good dog he was. And smart. He kept quiet the whole time. Questions echoed in her head. Would their hiding place be revealed to the smugglers as the smugglers removed the crates? Would they harm her and Jason if they did find them? How was her team of workers doing up at Burr Oak? And most important, where the heck was Sheriff Kane?

# Chapter Eleven

Dotty was scurrying around the kitchen. She was really starting to worry. *What is taking Penny and Jason so long?* Dotty thought as she glanced at the kitchen clock. It was 12:45, the open house was scheduled to begin at 1:00 and Penny and Jason were still gone. Dotty was concerned about Penny not being there to direct things. But more alarming was not knowing if they were in danger or not.

"Bitsy, gather everyone here," she said "I'm busy as a long-tailed cat in a room full of rocking chairs, but we need a little pow-wow......."

Bitsy went and did as bidden to notify Paul and Jackie. She was worried too. Bitsy was rather fond of Jason and not knowing what he was going through was beginning to fray her nerves. What would she do if anything happened to him? Her anxiety gave way to exasperation. Why weren't he and Penny returning? Just like a man to keep a gal wondering, she thought.

Soon the trio was in the kitchen, looking to Dotty expectantly. The self-appointed stand-in for Penny took one final look at the clock and began "You know how important this day is to Penny. Golly scissors, to all of us. We have worked hard to make this day happen. We've all had an important part to play in the preparation. Penny and Jason aren't back yet so... "

"We all know what to do, so let's do it." Then she added, "And don't forget to say a prayer for Penny and Jason."

No sooner had Dotty spoken than a car was heard pulling into the front driveway. "It starts," said Paul, and he and Bitsy filed out to attend to the customers. Jackie stayed to help Dotty take the refreshments to the table set up in the parlor.

Paul and Bitsy greeted the first guest at the door. "Welcome to Burr Oak Bed and Breakfast. My name is Paul Engelhardt."

"Thank you," she said looking around "My name is Lisa Clay. I work at the college."

"Oh, yes," Paul said "I thought you looked familiar. We will be giving a tour as soon as we have more people for a group. In the meantime, please help yourself to refreshments over here in the parlor. You are welcome to look around in there. Please sign our registration book."

# Chapter Twelve

The smugglers were busily loading up the crates from the cave onto their boat when the leader announced, "Got to go to the open house now. Ray, you and Yancy keep loading. I'll meet you tonight down river. I should be in time to help you unload after dark." He headed toward the cave opening. "I sure don't like doing this in broad daylight, but we had no choice. Had to do what the big boss said. Keep your guns handy."

The boss had gone, leaving, Ray and Yancy to continue the loading of the crates. His words had at least given Jason and Penny a warning that Ray and Yancy were armed.

*This is it*, was Penny's thought as the crate hiding them was removed. The one called Ray let out a yelp when he saw them. Then he grabbed for his weapon "Hey, Yance We got us some snoops here."

Yancy turned and seeing his partner's gun drawn, he pulled out his own gun and came closer.

"Alright folks Come on out of there," Ray demanded "Hands up and no funny business. We got two guns on you."

Jason and Penny looked at one another. *Well, this is a no-brainer.* They both stepped forward. Out of the corner of her eye, Penny saw Wang belly along the floor of the cave. He had been behind another small crate and the smugglers had not seen him. *Good luck, Wang – whatever you plan to do,* she thought. Because, you see, Penny had already learned that Wang was no ordinary dog. She was convinced that he had a plan and he would come through for them.

Ray and Yancy tied Jason and Penny's hands and feet. Gags had also been placed in their mouths. Penny now knew why it is called a gag. She tried not to think about where that dirty rag had been, which Ray had stuffed in her mouth. Soon Ray would finish loading the boat. Penny had to think of something. She tried to move her hands behind her back, but the ropes were so tight that her wrists were hurting.

Jason seemed to be in the same fix. Penny felt him move against her side as he tested his ropes, but they were as tight as hers were. Penny heard Ray talking to Yancy as he returned to the cave "Go on with the boat. You need to leave now to be able to get to the drop-off site," he explained to Yancy. "I've got these two snoops all trussed up like Christmas turkeys. They ain't going nowhere, "Sides, I got old reliable here," he said waving the handgun.

"Okay, Ray. If you're sure. I'll find out from the old man what he wants done with them."

With that parting and gloomy piece of news, Yancy was out the opening of the cave and soon they heard the sound of his boat leaving. Ray sat down across from Penny and Jason. "I'll just keep an eye on you two," he declared. "Not that you would be going anywhere. Ain't no one can tie better knots than I can."

Ray pulled a cigarette out of his shirt pocket, and balancing it between his teeth while he lit it, he continued to talk. "We'll just set here and have a little chat while I wait to hear back. Too bad you can't join in the conversation," he sneered "Ha ha."

Jason, evidently trying to respond, choked on his gag. He frowned at Ray, which was not a smart move on his part. Ray rose to his feet, brandishing his weapon. "So, mister smartie. You think you're better than me, don't you? I'll show you whose better, "Ray exploded, kicking Jason in the mid-section with his boot.

While Jason fought to recover his breath, Penny felt a tear slide down her cheek. *Poor Jason. What have I gotten us into? Oh, where is that sheriff anyway?*

After Yancy had left, Ray became much meaner. He seemed to enjoy having power over them. Now he turned to Penny and bending down close to her face, he demanded, "What's a matter, girlie? Whatcha bawlin' for?"

At a distance, Ray was not a pretty sight. His teeth were badly decayed and nicotine-stained. But up that close, he was totally disgusting. Penny closed her eyes, but he kicked her leg, demanding she open her eyes and look into the face of the one who held her life in his hands.

Penny opened her eyes in time to see the smuggler reach out and grab her hair. As he did, a large, light brown blur flew towards him. It knocked Ray off his feet and threw him against the wall where he hit his head. With a groan, he slipped down the wall into a heap on the cave floor, totally unconscious. It all happened so fast that Penny wasn't sure if she had imagined it or if it had really happened.

Ray's gun had been knocked from his hands and had fallen next to Penny's legs. She raised her feet and scooted it under her knees. The light brown blur came to Penny and fastening his teeth on the rag, pulled it out of her mouth Penny gasped as clean fresh air rush in. "Wang, you wonderful dog, you! I'm so glad you are here." They nuzzled cheeks.

They were interrupted by a grunt of protest from Jason. Penny grinned "Wang, do you suppose you could get that gag out of Jason's mouth too?"

Seeming to understand her completely, Wang began to pull the gag from Jason's mouth. Once Jason's mouth was free again Penny asked, "Are you okay, Jason?"

"Much better now with that stinking rag out. We've got to get untied before sweetie there comes to. Thanks, Wang. Good boy. Do you think you could untie our hands?"

Wang was already pulling at Jason's ropes when they heard a boat pull up in front of the cave. *Oh no*, Penny thought. *Yancy is back.*

That thought was quickly dispelled at the sound of Sheriff Kane's voice calling, "You in the cave. Come out with your hands up."

Jason groaned, "Give me a break."

"Sheriff, this is Penny Powers. We are tied up. One of the smugglers is unconscious. Come quick before he comes to."

Kane slowly entered the cave, gun drawn and pointing ahead. When he saw them, he stopped, his jaw dropped. "Where's the smuggler?" he asked.

Penny nodded her head towards the unconscious Ray. "Over there. He hit his head on the rocky wall when he fell," she explained.

"Fell? What happened to him?" Kane asked.

"Wang," Penny answered.

"Huh?" Kane asked.

"My dog, Wanger Doops. Wang jumped him as he was about to hit me and knocked him down. His name is Ray and he was pretty mean to us. He and his partner bound and gagged us and still he physically tormented us."

Kane looked first at Jason, then at Penny as he rose to come and untie them "Gagged, huh? And where are those gags now?" he asked doubtfully.

"Wang, again," Penny explained.

"Yeah, right, and just where is this remarkable dog? Invisible, is he?"

"He's right behind you."

Kane turned. Sure enough. There was Wang quietly standing behind the sheriff. "Humph," Kane grumbled and finished untying them.

To this day, Penny not sure if Kane believed that a dog named Wanger Doops knocked out a smuggler and freed them from their gags. But who knows? And given time, Wang might even have gotten them untied! Penny was convinced he could have.

Penny rose to her feet with difficulty. Her legs were stiff and her fingers were numb. Jason had not risen yet and she went to give him a hand.

It was obvious as he tried to stand that he was still in pain from Ray's boot to his middle. Penny helped him to get outside the cave. He could not straighten up and she knew he was suffering yet.

As they were getting their legs to working again, the sheriff returned from the boat where he had cuffed Ray to the side. He helped Jason out to the boat "I think we'd better get you to the clinic once we dock the boat, he said. "Might have some broken ribs or something. Suppose we better have the doc look at this smuggler, too"

# Chapter Thirteen

Soon they were on their way back to the county dock. They were quite a sight to behold, if anyone was beholding. The smuggler cuffed to the side of the boat, still unconscious; Jason doubled over and holding his abdomen as the bouncing boat caused more discomfort; Penny, well, she was pretty normal except her hair was a mess. And let's not forget the hero of the day, and that's not Sheriff Kane! No, Wang was the hero and he looked the part, too. Sitting in the very front of the boat, the wind blowing his ears back, he looked like was leading them all on a charge. In a sense, he had been. Penny thought, my hero, Wanger Doops!

Once back at the Sheriff's office, Ray refused to give his or Yancy's last name. He also refused to give up the boss, claiming he didn't know what the sheriff was talking about.

However, Sheriff Kane did give Penny and Jason some good news. Fingerprints revealed that Ray had lived a busy life of crime. He had been in prison twice for robbery and aggravated robbery. This third charge of aggravated robbery was likely to keep him off the streets for some time.

As for Yancy, who turned out to be Lou Yance, he was picked up down river. He also would not give up the name of their boss. Penny began to wonder if they even knew their boss's name. Penny remembered the conversations she overheard in the cave. Yancy had talked about the "old man." Penny sincerely hoped that the law would get them all and put them away.

The clinic was closed on Saturday afternoons, so the doctor came to the Sheriff's office to check on Jason. Matthew Whitman, MD had grown up in Gannon Ridge and after finishing medical school, had returned to Gannon Ridge to take up practice in the local clinic as a junior partner. His partner was an older doctor by the name of Ben Lewis. Ben was off this weekend on a fishing expedition, so Doc Whitman was the only one available.

Matt Whittman was a slender and muscular young man. His dark brown hair, parted on the side, allowed a curl or two to drop down over his eye. This seemed to be the cause for a habit of running his fingers through his hair to lift it away from his eyes.

Dr. Whitman pronounced Jason well enough to return home. No broken ribs, just some pretty sore muscles. There was, however, the possibility of damage to the spleen, so Dr. Whitman said he would have to be on bed rest for a couple of days and come in to see him at the clinic on Wednesday.

"He's coming to Burr Oak. It just so happens that I have an empty room," Penny said firmly. "That's the least I can do for you after what you went through."

Jason smiled sheepishly. "Yes, ma'am." He recognized from her tone of voice that there was no point in arguing with his boss.

Dr. Whitman gave Penny a small packet of pills saying, "Give Jason one of these if the pain gets worse, especially if he has trouble sleeping."

"Thank you, doctor," Penny said taking the packet. "And if he gets worse before Wednesday?"

He smiled and his eyes twinkled. Very blue eyes. "Then I'd better give you my card with my phone number so you can call me," he said handing his card to her. "Since you don't have a vehicle, why don't I give you a lift back to Burr Oak?"

"Thanks, that would be great," Penny said.

"By the way, congratulations on the opening of Burr Oak I was up there earlier for the open house Looks fantastic."

"The open house!" Penny exclaimed. "Horrors! I forgot all about it." She looked at her watch. It was 4:30. The open house had been over for ½ an hour.

"Jason, do you still have your cell phone? I need to call Burr Oak.'

"I do, Penny. But the battery is dead."

Sheriff Kane to the rescue "Here, Ms. Powers, you can use the desk phone."

"Thanks," Penny said. She picked up the receiver and dialed Burr

Oak.

"Burr Oak Bed & Breakfast," answered Bitsy.

"Bitsy, its Penny I'm sorry we - - - - "

"Penny, where have you been? Where's Jason? Is he okay? We were so worried. Why didn't you come back? Where are you? What...?" Bitsy's tirade had left Penny breathless. Certainly, she thought, Bitsy must be too.

"Jason and I are at the Sheriff's office. He, Jason, not the Sheriff, was injured by one of the smugglers - - - -." Penny was interrupted as Bitsy screeched, "Jason! Jason's hurt? Oh no! Oh my gosh!"

"As I was saying, Bitsy, Jason is okay, just needs some bed rest. Dr. Whitman is giving us a ride back to Burr Oak," she explained "And, Bitsy, get the room at the top of the stairs ready for Jason. He's supposed to be on bed rest so we will keep an eye on him there."

"Okay, Penny I'll get the room ready right now. You're sure Jason's going to be okay? You're not just trying to break it to me gently."

"Yes, Bitsy He's going to be okay. You can talk to him yourself soon. We'll be leaving in a few minutes," Penny said. Then added, "How was the open house?"

"It was great, Penny. But you just get Jason here and I'll tell you all about it then."

*Touché, I guess*, Penny thought.

Dr. Whitman assisted them into his Honda CRV. Exactly like Penny's, except his was blue "Nice Honda," Penny said.

"Oh, you like Hondas?" he asked.

"Oh, yes, it's just like mine except for the color," Penny said, thinking that Dr. Whitman's Honda matched the color of his eyes.

"Oh, what color is yours?" he inquired.

"Eyes," Penny returned dreamily.

"What?" he asked, puzzled.

"Hmmm? Oh, color, yes. It's grey," Penny said recovering her loss of sense. *Gee, Powers. Get a grip!*

He smiled. *A smile that could only go with those eyes*, Penny thought.

"Well, here we are," he said, pulling up to the big house. He helped Jason out of his Honda. As Penny aided them up the steps, the door suddenly burst open, and out came Bitsy in a rush. A veritable whirlwind.

# Chapter Fourteen

For the next couple of days, Jason lived the life of Riley. Bitsy was there to wait on him hand and foot. Even Wang sat guard, or laid guard, you could say, as he was found at times on the foot of Jason's bed. No one got to Jason unless he approved. Dotty cooked all Jason's favorites. In fact, he was so well taken care of that he had no time to actually rest. Everyone wanted to hear from Penny and Jason all the details of their little adventure in the tunnel under Burr Oak. Penny thought that must tire Jason the most. She finally had to put a do-not-disturb sign on the door so he could get some sleep. Wang stayed in Jason's room beside the bed. Penny knew Wang would let her know if Jason needed anything.

Penny wondered if the doctor meant for Jason just to lie down or did he mean for him to sleep also. Well, she did have his phone number on the card he gave her. She decided to call him. It was his cell phone; so of course, he was busy in the clinic and did not answer. She left a message.

"Dr. Whitman, this is Penny Powers," she said very officially. "I just had a question about Jason's bed rest. Well, really not rest. Actually, I guess I need a clarification on the rest part. What I mean is, someone is always in his room, talking or asking him about what happened. I was wondering if that is too much for him. I mean, did you want him to actually sleep when he rests or just not have company?"

*Well, that went pretty well*, she thought. *I'll just wait for his return call.*

An hour later, Dr, Whitman called "This is Matt Whitman, Penny I got your message about Jason," he began. Did she detect a smile in his voice? Penny didn't have a picture phone, but she could see his blue eyes just as clearly as if she did. "It's alright for Jason to have company as long as there is no rough-housing. You might allow him a one or two hour nap. And, of course, a good night's sleep."

"Thank you, Dr. Whitman," Penny said "I'll see to it."

"If you like, I could come out on my way home today and look in on him," he added "No extra charge."

"Oh, that would be great," Penny said, mentally going over her wardrobe "Perhaps you could stay to dinner with us," she added shyly.

"Okay, I'll do that. And Penny, you can call me Matt."

"Okay, Dr… uh ..Matt. I'll see you tonight."

As Penny replaced the receiver in the cradle, she began yelling. "Dotty, Dotty!" Penny raced into the kitchen. "The doctor is coming out after clinic hours to check on Jason."

"Jason!" interrupted Dotty. "What has happened? Is he worse? What's wrong?"

Bitsy, upon entering the kitchen and overhearing Dotty, took up where she left off. "Oh, I knew he should have been admitted to the hospital. I shouldn't have left him alone. I suppose he did something he shouldn't have while I wasn't with him."

"All right you two. Calm down. Jason is just fine. As I was saying before being interrupted, I asked Matt to dinner. What I wanted to know is if there is anything to serve for dinner."

Dotty tilted her head slightly. Why did she remind Penny of Wang when she did that? "Matt now, is it?" she said slyly.

"He doesn't want...well, he…, that is he asked me to call him Matt," Penny stammered.

"Uh huh," responded Dotty "Well, I have some of my Gannon Ridge Stew simmering. How does that sound?"

"Wonderful, Dotty!" Penny exclaimed. "Your stew is heavenly. And how about some of your melt-in-your-mouth biscuits to go with it?"

"Will do," she said. "Now you better go see to what .. well, check out what you'll be wearing. You're so all fired up, you'll probably have …….trouble picking something out. You'll want to look……well,….you know."

Penny looked at Dotty, thinking she must be funning with her, but her expression did not show that she was. Dotty had turned back to her kitchen work. So Penny scurried back to her apartment and began pulling things out of her closet and drawers. Finally deciding on dress slacks and a knit top, she was just putting the other clothes away when she heard a sound from the library.

Penny hurried down the hall, arriving at the library door the same time as Wang. A very slight and muffled sound came to Penny. Wang looked at her and back at the door. She quietly opened the door and they softly entered the room together.

Wang and Penny stood quietly in the center of the room looking at the fireplace. There was nothing out of the ordinary in the room. No sounds, nothing. But they both knew they had heard something. As Penny continued to stand there expectantly, she heard the front door chimes. That would be Matt.

Penny poked her head out of the library door just as Bitsy opened the front door and welcomed the doctor. Down the hallway, Matt saw her and she motioned for him to come. Penny put her finger to her lips for him to observe silence .Matt looked to each side, wondering why the need for silence, then putting his medical bag down, he proceeded down the hallway.

When Matt reached the library door, Penny whispered, "Wang and I both heard sounds in here. This is the room where the secret passageway opens. The entrance is through the fireplace.

Matt nodded and they entered the room. Wang was over by the fireplace, sniffing. Matt's blue eyes searched the room with a puzzled expression.

After sniffing the fireplace one final time, Wang slowly sauntered out of the room. "Well, guess whatever had been there is gone now if he is no longer interested," Penny said, and they left too.

"That's quite a dog you have there," Matt said. He knew that her dog had helped save hers and Jason's lives. "What's his name?"

"Wanger Doops. Wang for short. You must not have seen him at the Sheriff's office. I guess he went on home without waiting for us."

Matt laughed. "I thought when you said that you and Wang heard noises, that you had a Chinese cook or something." Penny laughed too. "But where did you come up with a name like Wanger Doops?"

"My grandmother had a dog with that name when she was young," Penny explained "She named him that after a popular song at the time,

The Wang, Wang Blues. In fact, we have the sheet music. Jason ordered it and he plays it every once in a while." Penny added, "Wang doesn't like the music though. He leaves the room when we play it."

"Guess he knows when you're even talking about it," Matt said.

"Huh?"

"Look," Matt nodded toward Wang.

Sure enough. Wang appeared to have both his paws over his ears.

"He really does seem to understand what we are saying. Nothing much gets by him," Penny said.

Penny took Matt up to Jason's room. She removed the do-not-disturb sign. It was redundant to have it there anyway because Bitsy was setting next to Jason's bed talking with him. When they entered, she jumped up and said, "I was just leaving to help Dotty with dinner, Penny." And she bounced out of the room.

"I'll leave you and the doctor alone, Jason," Penny said. "I'll be down stairs. Matt, come down when you are ready. Dinner will be waiting." She left the room, noticing out of the corner of her eye that Wang had positioned himself at the foot of Jason's bed.

*Hmmm*, she thought. *Wang must have heard the sounds in the library all the way up here and had gone down to investigate. He really is taking care of us here.*

"Jason is doing fine, "Matt said as he seated himself at the table in the dining room. "I don't think any damage was done to his spleen, but its best to be cautious."

At Burr Oak, Penny and her staff shared their meals together. They had been using the dining room since they weren't open for business yet. Once the guests were there, the staff would eat in the kitchen. Tonight they were entertaining company and so they all dined in the dining room.

Bitsy stayed long enough to eat her own meal and to talk with Matt about Jason. Then she prepared a food tray for Jason and took it up to him.

After she left, Paul snickered "I wonder if he feeds himself or if Bitsy does it." They all laughed but it was very evident to all of them that Bitsy was extremely fond of Jason.

"For the love of Pete, leave those two alone," admonished Dotty. "They're doing just fine without help from ……".

The evening was so nice that Penny made the suggestion she and

Matt go out on the big veranda "You really have a nice view from up here," Matt said.

"I know. I feel so fortunate that Uncle Harry left Burr Oak to me. It has taken a lot of money to fix it up and get it ready for a Bed & Breakfast, but I think it's worth it. It really wasn't in too bad a shape to begin with."

As the sun went down, Matt and Penny sipped on their iced herbal teas. He didn't seem to be in any hurry to leave. Penny was glad. She felt snug as a bug in a rug (another of Dotty's quips-oh dear) with Matt on the wicker settee next to her. That feeling was suddenly interrupted by the appearance of Wang.

Wang lumbered – yes, no other word would describe it. Wang lumbered across the veranda to their settee. He tried to nudge his way between them, but there was no room. When that didn't work, he flopped down at their feet. He sighed and groaned and made other sounds that only a dog could utter.

This was unbelievable. Wang was slowly losing his hero status in Penny's eyes. The final straw came when he proceeded to give himself a bath in the noisiest and most disgusting fashion she had ever heard or seen him do.

Penny guessed it was too much for Matt also, as he rose from his seat saying, "Well, I guess I'd better head home. I have a busy week ahead of me and this is only Monday. Thank you, Penny I had a nice evening. Thanks for dinner."

Penny rose too, rather reluctantly. "I'm glad you could stay for dinner and thanks for looking in on Jason," she said.

Penny walked with him to his Honda. Actually "they," as Wang was right there with them, having discontinued his bathing.

"Goodnight, Penny."

"Goodnight, Matt."

# Chapter Fifteen

"Land sakes alive, you'd think it was spring instead of fall," Dotty stated.

"How's that" asked Jackie.

"Bitsy's all lovesick over your brother. And now Penny......"

Jackie looked up from the cookies she was frosting. "Penny? What about Penny?"

Dotty looked exasperated. "You mean to tell me you didn't notice her all moony-eyed last night over the doc?"

"You're kidding! No, I didn't notice. Our Penny and Doctor Matt! Super!"

"Yeah, well it may be super to them...... but Wang's sure got his sniffer bent out of shape over it........ Darn fool dog wouldn't let them be after dinner. Tried to squeeze in-between them on the settee. He even tried washing his private parts...... and pretty noisy about it too"

Jackie smiled, "And you know all this took place because....?"

"Uh.......because I was checking on them. I don't just spend all my time in the kitchen, you know. I have other responsibilities here…and… and….one of them is looking out for our Penny...... among other things."

"And you do a fine job of it, Dotty," Jackie said giving Dotty a hug. "I don't know what Burr Oak would do without you."

"So," Jackie asked, "what should we do about Wang?"

"Guess we need to keep him busy with something else when Penny and Matt are together. That is if Matt comes again. Seeing that fleabag washing his behinder sure would chase away any romantic thoughts I might have," Dotty stated firmly.

"Oh, Dotty," laughed Jackie "You know Penny wouldn't allow a flea on Wang. Besides Matt is a doctor. With what he sees everyday, I doubt that a dog washing himself would chase away romantic thoughts of anyone like our Penny."

"You're probably right about Penny," said Dotty stomping her foot. "If he's worth his salt, he'll not be able to stay away from Penny......."

By the time the cookies were all decorated and the dishes done, the two of them had formulated a plan to keep Wang and Penny separated when Matt was around. They vowed to also enlist the aid of Bitsy. And if need be, the guys, but only as a last resort. "You know how weird guys tend to get...well... at the mere hint of matchmaking," cautioned Dotty.

The need for the help from the guys arose sooner than they expected.

That very next afternoon Penny entered the kitchen and announced to Dotty that she was going to pick Matt up from the clinic and take him to the auto shop to get his Honda back. He was having routine maintenance done on his Honda. "I'm taking Wang with me," Penny said, slipping her bag over her shoulder.

Dotty nearly choked as she blurted out, "No......No, you can't!"

"I can't?" Penny asked "Why not?"

"Because I need him. Err. That is he..I...we... have something for him to do. Now you just go right on with your plans. And I'll do what I ... need...with...Wang...to do."

Penny looked at Dotty quizzically. "Are you okay Dotty?"

"Yes, yes I'm fine. It's just that I uh ...need Wang to uh ...help me."

"But for goodness sakes Dotty. How can Wang help you?"

"It's the basement. Yes, that's it – the basement. I heard....something down there ...and ......and I need him to come with me."

"Well, don't go down there then. We don't use the basement anyway."

"No, I have to. Need to get it cleaned up. It's, it's uh, tornado, yes tornado season and.....and we need it for a storm shelter for guests. So I need to clean it now and ...and I need Wang to help. I mean to be there".........."

Penny shrugged her shoulders. "Okay, Dotty, but I don't want you doing that all yourself. I'll tell Bitsy, Jackie and Paul to help you." And jingling her car keys in her hand Penny went in search of those lucky three people.

"Well, Dotty. You sure did a good job of keeping them apart." Bitsy shuddered as a cobweb settled on her arm. "But getting us all involved in this hair-brained scheme was a little much."

"It still needed to be done …..for the guests. Don't know why I didn't think of it sooner."

Paul sat a box down and looked at them. Folding his arms across his chest he asked, "Okay out with it. You females are up to something. What 'hair-brained scheme? Who are you keeping apart?"

Bitsy rolled her eyes. "We may as well tell him. He won't leave us be until we do." Paul nodded his agreement with her statement.

"It's like this," Dotty explained "Wang doesn't want Penny and the Doc to be romantically involved and we are trying to keep Wang away from Penny when Matt is around and Penny was going to take Wang to pick up Matt and there you have it." Dotty stopped and took a deep breath, having actually said one whole sentence though a long one.

"There you have what? What are you talking about?" asked Paul.

"It was the best I could ..uh…think of to keep Wang here to… " she paused looking around. "Where is he anyway?"

"Who?"

"Wang! Who did you think we were talking about?"

Paul picked up the box again. "Well, we all got roped into this work for nothing," he said sheepishly "Wang was at the door pawing to get out, so I let him out. I didn't know about your devious little plans. So you see this work is all a waste of time."

Dotty snorted "Okay, so we'll try better next time. But it wasn't wasted. Still need the basement ….for a tornado shelter……"

"No, actually you don't. Didn't you notice the fallout shelter outside the kitchen? Jason and I had that all cleaned and stocked a couple of weeks ago. We don't need the basement."

Dotty and the girls stood looking at Paul. Jackie asked, "Did Penny know about it?"

"Sure. She's the one who told us to work on it," Paul answered.

"Oh, for mercy sakes." exclaimed Dotty "Let's get out of here!"

The job of cleaning out the basement was abandoned as the group tromped up the stairs, disappointed that their plan had gone awry. They reached the kitchen in time to hear the phone ringing.

# Chapter Sixteen

Penny left Burr Oak slightly confused by her interaction with Dotty. She was not sure she understood why Dotty wanted the basement cleaned for a storm shelter when the fallout shelter had already been restored. But then Dotty was always pretty sensible about things. Perhaps there was ordnance or something that Penny would not be aware of being from the city. Before leaving, she had instructed the rest of the team to help Dotty work in the basement.

Once Penny was in her Honda, she drove away from Burr Oak. As she drove down the road, which curved below Bur Oak, she was suddenly surprised by a flash out of the corner of her eye.

She slowed down just as a big, light brown dog leaped from the wooded hillside skidding to a halt at the edge of the road. Penny applied the brakes and found herself looking out her door at none other than Wanger Doops "Wang, what are you doing here? You're supposed to be helping Dotty."

There wasn't much point in taking Wang back. She would be late in picking up Matt. So Penny opened the passenger door. "Come Wang."

Wang didn't need the command. The opened door was enough of an invitation for him. Soon he was settled in his favorite spot – in the Honda next to Penny. "I guess I'd better let Dotty know where you are," Penny told Wang. She opened her cell phone and dialed Burr Oak. The answering machine came on the line.

"Dotty, this is Penny. I just wanted to let you know that Wang ran down the road to meet me, so I'll just keep him with me. Guess your basement critter scared him too. I'll see you later. Bye."

Penny didn't notice the look Wang gave her as she finished her message.

Penny tucked her cell phone in her purse beside her and reached over to gently scratch Wang behind the ears. "You look pretty pleased with yourself, fella," she said. "Guess I would too if I got out of cleaning that basement."

"We're going to go pick up Matt. He needs a ride. But you will have to get in the back seat when we pick him up."

As Penny was looking at the road ahead, she missed the reaction Wang had to her statement. As she pulled up in front of the clinic, Penny spied Matt. He was watching for her and gave a friendly wave when he saw her.

As Matt neared her vehicle, Penny turned to Wang and pointed to the back seat. "Wang, back seat," she said. But Wang did not respond. Instead, he sat on the front seat next to Penny looking straight ahead.

"Wang, come on. Get in the back seat." She took his collar and attempted to pull him in that direction. A low rumble sounded in Wang's throat. Penny took her hand away, disbelieving what she had heard.

Matt opened the door, but halted when he saw Wang. Penny rolled her eyes and said, "I'm sorry, Matt, but Wang seems pretty determined to stay in the front seat."

"That's all right, Penny. I'll just climb in the backseat." And he climbed in. Wang turned his head for just a second and looked at Matt, then directed his attention back to the front.

"I guess I should have taken him back to Burr Oak," Penny explained "I had already left when he came running down the hill. I figured I'd just take him with me."

"No problem. He's probably just a little jealous. Can't say as I blame him. I'd probably do the same if I were him." Matt looked in the rearview mirror, meeting Penny's eyes, his own blue eyes twinkling as he smiled.

Penny felt the heat rise in her cheeks. *Cool it, Penny*, she told herself. *You're as bad as a teenager.* Matt's left arm moved across the back of the seat as he leaned forward. His hand touched Penny's shoulder and he gave her a little pat. He caught her eye and nodded toward Wang. Penny followed his look. *I can't believe Wang. That crazy dog looks downright mournful.*

"Penny, do you have time to make another stop before we go to the auto shop?' Matt asked.

"Why, yes I'm in no hurry to get back."

"Good. Then let's go to the Ice Crème Shoppe Do you know how to get there?"

Penny did know, and soon she was pulling into the parking lot in front of the Shoppe.

It was a nice little walk-up shop, popular with young and old alike. There were umbrella-shaded tables along the riverbank, creating a pleasant place to enjoy a tasty treat and the lazy river scene that afternoon.

As Matt disembarked from the Honda, he said to the dog, "Wang, want some ice cream? My treat."

Wang sprang to life. Matt had found the way to this dog's heart. It was through his stomach and it was with ice cream. Penny was happy Matt had taken the time to make friends with her dog. That made him pretty special in her eyes.

As the afternoon wore to a close, Matt spent more time with Wang. They played catch with a stick. Wang was having the time of his life. He was a happy dog and when Matt asked Penny to join them in their frolicking, he was nearly delirious with happiness.

When Matt announced that he really needed to get to the auto shop before they closed, they picked up their ice cream dishes and placed them in the trash. As Penny opened the driver's door, Wang jumped in and climbed into the back seat. Penny's eye caught Matt's. They both smiled, knowingly.

As they drove to the auto shop, Wang sat straight up in the back seat, looking for all the world like he had accomplished something great.

When Penny and Wang returned to Burr Oak, she let Wang out and he went bounding off into the woods. Penny went inside and made her way to the kitchen. The staff was just setting down to dinner. She observed that Dotty's expression appeared a little down. In fact, the rest of the staff showed evidence of the same mood.

As they finished eating, Penny rose and began clearing the table. "What a nice day it was today," she said, introducing the topic "Oh, by the way. Thanks for trying to watch out for me. Wang started out to be a pest, but Matt soon had him eating out of his hand. But, Dotty. The basement? Now really!"

# Chapter Seventeen

Penny's personal life had become a busy one. She and Matt were seeing each other on a regular basis. Everyone at Burr Oak had come to know and like Matt. He often would eat breakfast with Penny and the guests before going on to the clinic. They all enjoyed him and believed that he and Penny made a good match.

Matt's hobby was horticulture. In fact, he liked to relax from a stressful day at the clinic by working with flowers on the grounds at Burr Oak. The fact that the flowerbeds were always in bloom was in no small part due to Matt's work.

When the Bed & Breakfast opened for business, everything went off without a hitch. Four of the five rooms were occupied the first weekend. Advertising had gone well. Dotty preformed gastronomic miracles in the kitchen. More than ever, Penny was thankful for the day when Dotty had come to Burr Oak. The four young people were such an asset to the running of the business. They had all worked hard in getting the Bed & Breakfast up and going. Penny was very proud of her little "family."

As time passed and they were kept busy with the work and the guests, Penny and her staff forgot about the smugglers and the missing leader. Ray and Yancy were tucked safely behind bars. Nothing more was heard about those events on the day of the open house.

Even though Penny missed the event herself, the open house had been a success. A television news crew from a nearby city had given a very nice story covering Burr Oak, its history and its future. Since the owner had been "unavoidably detained" from appearing at the open house, the television station had called her and had added the telephone interview to the story.

Newspaper articles from several nearby towns had also covered the opening. Even towns in neighboring state of Wisconsin had newspaper coverage. Several bookings were made the day of the open house and many more came in the days to follow. It was official. They were definitely in business.

Dotty and her husband had moved into the carriage house apartment and Ed was working on changes there. Ed had also begun renovations on the shop below them. Paul and Jason were helping him now that the Bed & Breakfast was up and running.

Since it was nearing Thanksgiving, Penny decided not to open *The Tea Cozy* until spring. That would give them plenty of time for the renovations. Penny and her staff could still start herb seedlings in mid-winter and have plants from the nursery for customers by the time they opened in the spring. From the herb garden, she had already begun harvesting and drying herbs for her special tea blends.

Penny enjoyed her guests very much. She made it a point to have breakfast with them in the dining room. All the guests were served breakfast as part of the overall package. Additional meals were extra and they had to give a day's notice. Or there was Dotty's ever-popular box lunch for which most of the sightseeing guests requested.

Once the guests had sampled Dotty's delicious menus, they usually arranged to have one evening meal during their stay. Saturday was the one evening meal available to Bed & Breakfast weekend guests. During the week, arrangements could be made in advance for group parties. Penny anticipated that Christmas time would cause the number of those bookings to increase.

Most of the guests ended up hiring Jackie to do caricatures for them. She was a hit.

All in all, Penny deemed the Bed & Breakfast a success. She valued the friendships of her staff. The four young people continued to work on new marketing ideas, artwork, and ads for Bed & Breakfast services and also the plans for the upcoming opening of *The Tea Cozy*. In other words, everyone was very busy.

Even though the entire staff at the Bed & Breakfast was very busy, there was one member of the Burr Oak household, however, who did not appear to the casual observer as being very busy. In fact, Wanger Doops seemed to be pretty laid back. He could be found anywhere in the house or on the veranda sleeping.

"Wang sure sleeps a lot these days," was the general consensus among the staff. Penny had even taken Wang to the vet to see if he was ill. Dr. Warren could find nothing wrong with Wang. "He's in great shape," doc said "But maybe he's not sleeping at night. Are you aware of his night-time activities?"

"Wang usually sleeps in my bedroom," Penny replied "I'm not sure if he sleeps the whole night through or not." She vowed to check it out that very night.

Later that day, Paul had brought in the mail to the kitchen. Penny had set up a desk with a computer in the large kitchen for staff to use for Burr Oak business. Bookings were done there. Paul laid the mail on the desk and went back outside to work.

Soon a loud crashing sound followed by a dog howling was heard from the direction of the kitchen. Penny came running from her apartment, Dotty from the parlor, and the girls from upstairs where they were cleaning guestrooms.

Upon arriving in the kitchen, they found Wang lying on the floor in front of the computer desk, the overturned chair on top of him, along with papers and mail from the desk. As he scrambled, trying to get out from under the mess, Penny lifted the chair off of him.

"What is going on? Screaming like banshees in here! Wanger Doops! You bad dog," Dotty declared with her hands on her hips as she viewed his destruction "Golly whiz, just look at this mess …….. It'll take a month of Sundays to clean up!"

"That's okay, Dotty. We will lend a hand," said Penny.

"What was he doing?" asked Bitsy.

"Darned if I know," Dotty answered "Old scalawag…..! And me as busy as a long-tailed cat in a room full of rocking chairs."

"Now what's he doing?" asked Jackie. All eyes turned to Wang. He was viciously attacking one of the letters that had arrived in the mail.

"Wang, stop," called Penny as Bitsy made a dive to save the letter from Wang.

"Forever more," said Dotty "What do you suppose has gotten into him? He's sure acting......"

Penny opened the letter and found a cashier's check for a reservation that had been made earlier by phone. This one had been unusual because it had been for the entire week. Penny had said they would need prior payment for that length of time. This was the payment.

"Silly dog, could have lost us a wad of money," stated Dotty, giving Wang one of her looks that everyone had come to fear. Even Wang turned with head down and slowly walked out of the room. At the door he turned and looked back at Dotty, as if to see if her expression had changed. It hadn't and he left the kitchen.

"Wonder what that was all about," murmured Penny "That's not like him. Maybe Doc Warren is right. Maybe he's not sleeping at night and is getting weird during the day. Well, tonight I'll shut my door so I'm sure he stays in all night."

Even though Penny watched Wang all night, he did not move from her bed. She was baffled as to what had been the problem. The next few nights he stayed sleeping in her room. He seemed to require less sleep during the day. She perceived that he may have just been a little under the weather and was now on the mend.

# Chapter Eighteen

Monday dawned gloriously. It was a prime example of an Iowan Indian Summer day. Penny loved this kind of weather. She hated to see winter coming. She had been warned that some of the Iowa blizzards could be even worse that her New England winter storms.

Though Penny dreaded winter, she did look forward to the festiveness of the Christmas season. She had already begun planning the transformations that would occur at Burr Oak.

It was with these thoughts that she told her staff that she would be working with the herbs and nursery. Matt had Monday mornings off and he planned to come and work with her. Bitsy and Megan could handle the phone reservations and checking the new guests when they arrived, so she was free to work out there for the next couple of days.

"Good morning, Matt," Penny said cheerily as Matt climbed out of his Honda. "It's a fine morning for working with plants."

"Hi, Penny. Sure is and look here what I have in the back," he said as he opened the back of the Honda.

"Oh, Matt," Penny exclaimed. "This will work great for the wreaths. Where did you get it?"

As Matt picked up the velvety red ribbon he explained. "Stopped by *Millie's Flower Shop* yesterday. Thought we should have some nice stuff to make the wreaths with. It wasn't very expensive."

"That is super," Penny said "Thank you so much"

"Dotty brought a breakfast tray out to the nursery," Penny explained. "So we can eat as we go and save time."

"Dotty's scones and your herbal tea. Hmmm good!" said Matt "I never used to drink tea of any kind, let alone herbal but you've changed all that. You just have a way with those dried herbs."

"Thanks" said Penny "Glad you like it. But I think Dotty's scones would make anything taste good."

While Penny and Matt were working in the nursery that morning, Jackie was busy checking in the new guest who was to be there for the entire week. Mr. Jerrold Smith was a writer from Baton Rouge, Louisiana. He stated that he was here doing research on an upcoming book.

"That's interesting," Jackie said "What sort of book?"

"Oh, uh. Just general interest, I guess," Mr. Smith replied. "Could you show me where my room is? I'd like to get to work."

Jackie complied with his wishes and asking no more questions of him, she led Mr. Smith to his room. He had requested the Antebellum Room when he had registered by Internet. This was the room in which Jason had recuperated - at the top of the stairs above the library.

Later, as Jackie returned to the kitchen, she said to Dotty and Bitsy, "Smith sure is a cold fish. Doesn't want to talk at all. He just wants to do his research for his book."

"Well, maybe that's how authors are," replied Bitsy.

"I suppose he'll be late for meals and demand to be served at odd times," grumbled Dotty "Well, I won't be catering to any special whims of his just 'cuz he's an author, and that's final! I'm busy enough. I'll be working till the cows come home."

"I don't think we'll have to worry about that too much," explained Jackie. "I've already explained the rules to him. He doesn't even want to eat breakfast in the dining room, but has ordered a box lunch for breakfast and lunch each day. He paid in cash." Jackie held up the money to verify what she was saying.

"Sociable guy, too," murmured Dotty "You should have seen how rude he was to poor Mrs. Thomas. All she did was wish him a good morning. He practically bullied his way past her."

"Is that him?" asked Bitsy, looking out the kitchen window. She was looking at a man walking behind the house.

"Yes, that's him," responded Jackie as she and Dotty joined Bitsy at the window.

"You know, I believe I remember him from the open house," said Bitsy. "Quiet as a church mouse. Kept going off on his own. You're right,

Dotty. He wasn't very sociable then either."

"What's that he's got in his hand?" asked Dotty.

"Guess it's his notebook for his research," Jackie answered "Yes, see. He's writing in it right now."

"Humph," said Dotty, turning back to her work. But a commotion outside caused her to turn back to the window.

"Look at Wang," Bitsy exclaimed. "What has gotten into him?"

For Wang was walking in circles around Mr. Smith, barking. Smith attempted to scare the dog away by waving his notebook at Wang. "Get away, you stupid dog!" Smith snapped. But Wang continued to walk circles around him and bark.

Upon hearing the ruckus, Paul arrived on the scene. He took Wang by the collar and tried to quiet him. "Settle down, Wang," he admonished the rowdy dog "What's the matter with you?"

"Keep that dog away from me while I'm a guest here or you can refund my money," Smith demanded unpleasantly.

"Yes, sir. We'll make sure he is out of the way," Paul promised. Paul took Wang into the house, but not without some difficulty.

"Boy, Wang. You sure are being a pest," Paul said. He took Wang back to Penny's apartment and shut the door. Dotty and the girls helped him as he came out her door. "There," said Paul "I'd better go tell Penny what's up.

"Wang did that?" exclaimed Penny after hearing Paul describe Wang's behavior. "I just don't know what to think about him. I'd better go in and talk to him, Matt."

"Okay, it's time for me to get to the clinic anyway, Penny," Matt said giving her a goodbye kiss. "I'll see you later."

"Bye, Matt. Thanks for the ribbon and the help. It's fun working on this stuff with you."

Penny went to her apartment by the back way. As she opened the door, Wang burst through the opening and was soon disappearing into the woods before Penny could even think to call him. She stood looking at the spot in the woods where Wang had disappeared. *Well, that was certainly an intelligent thing to do*, she admonished herself. *Just open up the door and let him right out!*

Although Penny called, Wang paid her no heed and continued on. When the day drew to a close and she was ready to retire for the night, Wang had still not returned. Penny began to worry about him.

During the day Mr. Smith had not been around. Penny was thankful for that since Wang was on the loose. But now that the day was over her concern was evident. *Where is that rascal and more important, what is he up to?*

Dotty had informed her that Smith was 'holed up in his room.' They hoped he stayed there as long as Wang was out and about.

"Goodness" Penny said to no one in particular. "It's going to be a long week."

# Chapter Nineteen

That evening, a commotion arose at the sheriff's office. "Randy, what's all that racket outside?" demanded Sheriff Kane. The honking horns, voices and barking had drawn him from the back room.

Deputy Randy Thompson was standing at the window looking out onto Main Street watching the scene unfold. "Looks like that dog of Penny Powers is setting in the middle of the street. He won't let the cars past."

Kane reached the window as Wang was racing from car to car, barking furiously. "Wonder what he's up to now," murmured the Sheriff.

The sheriff and his deputy entered the street. Kane called the dog. Wang stopped barking when he heard his name and looked at the sheriff and his deputy. Suddenly Wang leaped onto a floral decoration and sent it tumbling onto the street. Kane yelled at Wang and made an attempt to go after him.

Wang, seeing he had pursuers, took off down the street, eluding the law officers by just enough to keep ahead of them. Kane saw that Wang was heading along the river toward the smuggler's cave. Using his communicator he said to his deputy, "Randy, go back and get the launch. Go down to the cave, but stay back so that your engine won't be heard. I've got a hunch about this. I want you to keep an eye on the cave. I think he's headed up the tunnel. I'm going on up to Bur Oak."

"Okay, Sheriff. I'll get right on that," Randy answered. With that said, Randy headed back to get the sheriff's launch and Kane got his cruiser and headed for Burr Oak.

Penny woke up with a start. She had been dreaming that she was lost in the woods and was being attacked by a pack of wolves. The howling she heard when she was awakened was no dream, however. It was real and was coming from inside the house.

Donning her robe, she made her way down the hallway. It didn't take Penny long to ascertain that the howling was originating in the library. And that the culprit was none other than Wanger Doops. Thinking of the sleeping guests, Penny said in an elevated whisper, "Wang. Please be quiet."

She attempted to open the library door, but it was as if someone was holding it shut. Suddenly, Penny was able to open the door and she burst into the library. The sight that met her eyes as she switched on the light caused her to gasp. For just inside the door was Wanger Doops, front paws on top of the unconscious Jerod Smith. Behind them was the gaping opening in the fireplace. She quickly took in the other details: the items in the tunnel and the remaining items next to the fireplace in the library itself. It was obvious that Smith was robbing them while they all slept.

Voices could be heard at the front of the house Penny peered down the hallway. Dotty, dressed in her nightclothes and robe, was entering the front door and behind her came Sheriff Kane.

"Oh, Dotty," said Penny with relief "I'm so glad you called the sheriff."

"Oh, I didn't call him," explained Dotty "He was just pulling up in front as I came out of the carriage house. I woke up when I heard Wang screaming like a banshee. Fool dog near woke the dead. What's he doing…?"

"Looks like Wang caught another smuggler. He's got him in here."

Sheriff Kane pushed his way into the library ahead of Dotty and Penny "Alright folks. Better step back and let the law take over." He spoke into his communicator, "Randy, we got the smuggler here at Burr Oak. You can take the boat back to the dock. See you back at the office."

Kane knelt beside the now semi-conscious Smith and placed handcuffs on him. He looked at Wang and said, "Good work, fella."

"Alright, Smith, or whatever your name is. On your feet. We've got a nice little cot just waiting for you down at the jail."

Smith groaned then pointed at Wang and said, "Keep that wild animal away from me! I'll sue!"

"Smith you won't be suing anyone, least of all these good folks," Kane said "On your feet."

As Sheriff Kane drove off with his prisoner, Dotty said "golly scissors!"

"Yup" agreed Penny. "That pretty much says it. Come here, Wang. Our hero. What a good dog you are."

Dotty turned and headed to the kitchen calling over your shoulder. "Come to the kitchen, Wang. You deserve a heroic bowl of ice cream."

With a yip Wang scooted ahead of Dotty and was waiting expectantly in the kitchen when she got there. After all, ice cream was his favorite treat.

# Chapter Twenty

Two days later, Matt and Penny were setting on the front porch reading the newspaper. On the front page was a picture of Wang along with a picture of Burr Oak. The headlines read:

*Local Dog Solves Smuggling Case*

The article expounded on Wang's heroic actions that resulted in the arrest and conviction of the gang of smugglers in the small Iowa town of Gannon Ridge. Penny was so proud of him. She read the article to Wang.

"We all knew what a hero Wang was. It's nice to know the newspaper recognized it too."

After a few minutes of quietly enjoying each other's company, Matt spoke.

"You know, this isn't bad."

Penny glanced at Matt. They were seated on the swing on the veranda the one facing the setting sun. It was starting to get a little chilly for veranda-sitting, but the day had been an extra nice day. Penny had been thinking about how nice it was to be setting here with Matt. She glanced at his profile. He was so strong and handsome.

Penny's thoughts had been dwelling on him a lot lately. She was thinking in terms that they were getting to be much more than good friends. So when he made that statement her mind posed a question. *Did he mean being here with me or is it something in that silly paper he's been glued to?*

"What isn't bad?" She asked aloud.

With a twinkle in his merry eyes Matt slid closer to Penny putting his arm across her shoulder. He leaned close and softly spoke in her ear "It's not bad being romantically involved with a woman whose dog is top item in the newspapers and television reports." He leaned closer and gave her a kiss on the forehead, then settled back to the newspaper.

Penny's heart had been doing tumultuous flip-flops as Matt had leaned closer and whispered in her ear. But with his final statement her cloud nine seemed to plummet all the way to the ground. She jumped to her feet and stood looking down at him on the swing, her hands on her hips.

"And just what makes you think we are romantically involved, Matthew Whitman?"

Matt slowly folded the paper and placed it on the side table. He took her hand and pulled her to the seat beside him. Taking both her tiny hands in his big strong hands he said, "What makes me think we are romantically involved is that I am about to tell you this: I love you Penelope Powers, with all my heart. And I am asking you to become my wife so that we can spend the rest of our lives being romantically involved together."

Well, that fairly melted Penny in her tracks, or in the swing. She could hardly catch her breath to speak. The words would not come.

"Well, Miss Powers What is your answer? Will you marry me?"

Wordlessly Penny nodded. But then words aren't really needed on some occasions.

One could almost believe the blissful smile on the face of the happy canine lying on the veranda just far enough back not to be seen by the two young people in love.

# Chapter Twenty-one

The next morning Penny was up bright and early. She was bouncing around the big house so full of bubbly cheerfulness that she was getting on Dotty's nerves.

"Penny, for the love of Pete! Will you go somewhere else and let me get on with my work? You can't even set still."

"I'm sorry, Dotty. I'm just so happy and so excited and so..." Penny dreamily held her hand out and looked at her engagement ring.

"Let me see that ring again," said Dotty wiping her hands on her apron. "Sure is a perty thing."

"Oh, Dotty," Penny said. "I'm so happy! I'm so glad that I left the city. It was so lonely there. Now I have a family-you folks, and I'm engaged to be married. I'm the happiest girl alive." Penny hugged Dotty warmly.

"Okay, okay... Time for me to get back to work. Why don't you go snip me some fresh rosemary for my red potatoes? Get on with you now." Dotty shooed Penny out of her kitchen.

As Penny headed through the kitchen's swinging door into the dining room she saw the Sheriff's pickup pull up in front. She went to the door wondering what brought him back so soon.

"Mornin', Penny," he said tipping his hat. "Got some surprising news for you."

"Come on in, Sheriff. I'll have Dotty bring us some tea and scones." Penny knew that was probably one of the sheriff's reasons for coming.

Once Sheriff Kane had the tea and one of Dotty's raspberry scones in hand he went on to state his main reason for coming.

"It seems that Smith wasn't as loyal as his partners in crime," he stated. "Once Smith realized where he was going and for how long, he gladly gave up the name of the boss." Kane leaned forward, looking intently at Penny. "And you'll never guess who the big guy was!"

"You mean it's someone we know?" asked Penny.

"Yup." The sheriff took another bite of scone. "Henry Meggers."

Shocked silence followed this revelation. Penny didn't know what to say. It was unbelievable.

"Took me by surprise too," said the sheriff. "But I guess Meg had the opportunity to test out the lay of the land, so to speak. Actually, this wasn't the only town along the River where Meg was spearheading the smuggling operations. He had Burr Oak pretty much cased just by the fact that it was empty and he had a good reason for being in the area. The cave along the river was perfect for them. He let it get around that he was interested in purchasing Burr Oak and therefore no one thought twice about his being in the area. Don't know how he figured out about the cave. No one here in Gannon Ridge seemed to know it ever existed."

"Woof!"

"Well, except for Wang here," the sheriff amended. He scratched Wang's right ear. Wang turned his head, presenting his left ear instead.

"Oh, sorry, Wang. Wrong ear."

Sheriff Kane paused to take another bite of his scone and wash it down with herbal tea. "Mighty fine scones," he said. When he was finished and saw that the one scone was all he would be getting, he rose and said, "Well, got to get back to the office. Plenty to do yet."

Penny rose also and shook his hand saying, "Thank you Sheriff. I appreciate your coming up here to tell me this information. I'm saddened to hear that it was Meg who was involved in this smuggling ring. I guess you just never know. Goodbye, Sheriff, and thanks again."

As Sheriff Kane pulled out of the circle drive, Penny pondered her experience at Meg's diner when he had reacted so strangely to her Bed & Breakfast plans. *No wonder*, she thought. *He was afraid I would get in the way of his smuggling operation.*

# Chapter Twenty-two

"Dotty! Where's the sign for the front door? I can't find it! It's almost time to open and I can't find it!" Penny was frantically scurrying all over the little shop called *The Tea Cozy*, turning things upside down looking for the grand opening sign.

Dotty shook her head and rolled her eyes "Gosh all fishhooks, Penny, now I know why the….the open house for the Bread and Breakfast went so well. Now don't take this wrong, but ……if you had been there and acting like this, we …..well, we would all have been….well, you know. Land sakes! Running around here like a chicken with its head cut off."

Dotty took Penny's hand and led her out the door of *The Tea Cozy*. There in front of the shop was the elusive sign, having been placed there by Paul and Jason earlier in the morning.

Penny, looking somewhat chagrined, said, "I'm sorry, Dotty. I guess I just don't do well when I'm stressed."

"Humph, I sure don't know why. Look at how calm you were when that smuggler had you captive. Don't see how… liked to have scared the puddin' out of me worrying about …well… you know……" Dotty, as usual was at a loss for words; some words that is. "Now take a deep breath and relax. Go sit down and have a cup of tea. The specialty of the day is brewing and ready."

Encouraged to take the time to do one of her favorite things, Penny went back into *The Tea Cozy* and poured herself a steaming cup of herbal tea. It was one of her own blends; one she had concocted during the winter months with her dried herbs. She had named it Gannon Ridge Sage, though of course, it had other herbs in it. Penny had wanted to name it something with Burr Oak in the name. Matt, however, said people might think it was made out of the oak trees that surrounded the big house. After a good laugh, they both agreed that the town name would be a better sell.

How soothing the tea was and Penny was soon dreamily recalling the past winter and all that had been accomplished. The bed and breakfast was a huge success. The rooms were surprisingly filled every weekend. A nearby skiing hill developed by a neighboring town to bring in tourist business during the winter had certainly been a help to her business.

The Christmas season was the happiest that Penny could remember. Not only did her little "family" at Burr Oak prove a joy to her, but the townsfolk also showed her what Iowa small town life is like at Christmas time.

There was the living nativity that the town had asked Penny to have on Burr Oak grounds. She felt privileged when they also asked her to play the part of Mary. The local Community church put on a musical drama for the community. Penny had been thrilled to see so much musical and acting talent in such a small town. Jason was a part of it. With his musical ability, he was a shoe-in to be part of the cast and even helped to direct it. Tourists who were staying at the bed and breakfast also attended the drama. The guests were transported to the church by horse-drawn sleighs complete with bells. *Thankfully there was plenty of snow for the sleighs*, thought Penny. *Note to self: look into the feasibility of having our own horses for our guests.*

The guests went home telling their friends that it was the most wonderful Christmas holiday they had enjoyed for a long time "That little town in Iowa really knows how to observe the birth of the Christ, and we were treated like royalty," they told their friends back home.

Penny spent a great deal of time with Matt throughout the holidays. Since their engagement, they were seen everywhere together. The townsfolk would whisper to one another when they saw Matt and Penny "Yup. Best thing that every happened to Dr. Matt was Penny Powers coming to town."

Though they had not set a date, Penny and Matt however, were planning for it and who would have a part of their special day. The business of getting the bed and breakfast off the ground and then the grand opening of *The Tea Cozy*, did not seem an appropriate time to be having a wedding. Once this was going and all the business problems weeded out, they knew they would *get down to brass tacks*, as Dotty would say. Penny wanted to be able to devote her whole self to preparing for her wedding. And Matt agreed that it would be good to wait.

Linda Booth and Penny had become fast friends. She and Jerry had already delivered the Booth Kettle Corn to the shop for the opening today and they continued to sell their corn product at *The Tea Cozy*. Marketing had also included their business with a link from the B & B's web page.

Penny drained the last from her teacup. She was happy with how the Gannon Ridge Sage blend had turned out. It was a pleasing and relaxing flavor; one that was best enjoyed in the morning along with one of Dotty's delicious scones.

*Well, I think I'm calmed down now,* thought Penny. *Time to get to work.*

# Chapter Twenty-three

The evening following the grand opening for the shop found the staff relaxing in the parlor of the bed and breakfast Dotty sat in a stuffed chair with her feet up on the ottoman. Penny also sat with her feet up. It was apparent that even though they were all exhausted, that they were happy with the outcome of *The Tea Cozy's* grand opening.

Bitsy voiced the question that everyone was thinking. "Why are we more exhausted from today than we were from the bed and breakfast grand opening?"

"I'm sure I don't know," said Dotty "But right now I think I'd better see if we have something to make sandwiches with. I'm sure everyone is famished."

They all nodded agreement and in one mind all got up to assist Dotty with preparing something to eat. As they made their way to the kitchen, they were interrupted by the sound of a honking horn out front

"It's Matt!" exclaimed Bitsy, observing the young doctor through the dining room window. "What on earth is he up to?" The rest of the group was drawn to the dining room window to see what Bitsy was talking about.

Bitsy's question was soon answered as Matt began hauling sacks and boxes out of his Honda. As they held the door open, it was obvious from the aroma that Matt carried food. They helped him take it all into the dining room. The group had suddenly become ravenously hungry at the sight of food being served to them with no work involved.

"Matt, this is so nice of you. But it seems like a lot of food," Penny said giving him a hug.

"Well, I know everyone has been working hard and not just today for this grand opening. I figured you needed some pampering tonight, especially Dotty. I didn't know what everybody liked so I stopped at a few different take-out places." Matt sat the last sack on the table and stood back beaming.

Ed came in, and smelling the food, went to the table to check it out "Well, what do we have here? Mexican, pizza, broasted chicken, and Chinese. I came just in time," he said.

"Well, grab a plate everyone and take whatever appeals to you. Gosh all fishhooks! Looks like Dr. Matt has taken care of us all," said Dotty.

As they all sat around the big oak dining table, Penny looked around at her friends. Dolly and Ed were discussing the day's work. Jason was asking Paul if the door to *The Tea Cozy* had been locked for the night. Bitsy was talking to Megan regarding continued marketing for both Burr Oak and *The Tea Cozy*.

Unconsciously Penny sighed. Her staff, her friends; they were a special family. Matt setting next to her leaned over and whispered in her ear, "A penny for your thoughts, Penny."

She smiled and said, "Just thinking how much I am blessed."

"Am I included in that blessing?" Matt asked her with a twinkle in his eye. He was still seated at the table.

Penny rose from her seat to go retrieve some more chicken. She leaned over and quietly said in his ear, "You know you are. A very special part." Penny planted a light kiss on Matt's forehead.

Matt squeezed her hand. "We all are blessed, Penny. It's hard to believe that all this has taken place in less than a year. I'm sure glad you decided to move to Gannon Ridge."

"Ditto that," said Dotty "Ed and I have been blessed a whole lot by you moving here, Penny. Not just the job and the apartment, but a family…you know…all of you….like the family we never had. Right, Ed?" Looking to her spouse for confirmation she wiped a tear from her eye with the corner of her apron.

Ed gave his wife a warm hug "Right you are, Dotty. Don't know quite how to thank you for all you've meant to us – every one of you."

Bitsy rose from the table. She took her pop can and tried banging a serving spoon against it. "I'd like to make a toast. Everyone raise their glasses, or whatever."

Glasses, bottles and pop cans were raised expectantly as the little group waited for Bitsy's toast.

"To Penny. She gave us a part of her business by allowing us to have shares in the Bed & Breakfast and *The Tea Cozy*. Penny has become such a good friend to all of us. Myself, I feel like she is a sister to me," as an afterthought, she added with a smile, "An older sister."

"To Penny," responded Matt with raised glass. "The love of my life."

"Hear, hear," was Jason's response as they all clinked their drinks. "Best employer ever!"

Penny was embarrassed "You guys, this all wasn't necessary, but I appreciate your feelings. You made it easy for me to work with you all. You're all like family to me too. Correction. You are family. As for the business, you have worked so hard to make it come about, it only seems right that you have shares in it."

Later, having finished her chicken, Penny rose to start cleaning up. "I don't know about the rest of you, but I'm exhausted and ready to hit the sack. Let's get the leftovers put away and put the dishes in the sink. "No, Dotty," she said seeing Dotty about to object. "There aren't that many and for once we will retire for the night with some dirty dishes in the sink."

So the little family from Burr Oak took their utensils to the kitchen, placed them in the sink, and stored the leftovers in the refrigerator. After everyone else had left, Matt and Penny stood at the front door in each other's arms. "Penelope Powers," Matt breathed softly in her ear. "I love you."

"I love you, Matt Whitman," Penny said with her head on his shoulder.

After a final goodbye kiss, Matt left for his Honda and drove out the driveway heading towards his home in town. Penny closed the front door, and made her way back to her apartment. Wang followed close at her side. "I guess it's been a busy day for you too, huh Wang?" She massaged him behind the left ear. "What a good boy you have been. And a great companion. I am really glad you …I…well, whichever one of us found the other, I'm glad."

Wang whined in delight. Was it from the massage or because he agreed with Penny's statement? Who knows?

## Chapter Twenty-four

It was business as usual for the B & B and *The Tea Cozy*. Several weeks had passed and the wedding plans were continued.

"Penny, I just had the strangest phone call," Jackie exclaimed, bursting into the parlor. "I don't know what to make of it."

"Who was it from?" asked Penny.

"Sheriff Kane," was her answer.

"Well, what did he want?" she asked.

"Just wanted to know if you were at home. When I said yes, did he want to talk to you; he said to make sure you didn't leave. He'd be right out."

"I wonder what that is all about," said Dotty. "Man sure can be strange sometimes."

"Yes, Sheriff Kane has a different way of working with things," said Penny. "But Dotty, he sure does like your scones! Better make sure you have one or two when he comes out."

Dotty merely grunted her response.

Later, as Sheriff Kane was being seated with a cup of tea and one of Dotty's blueberry scones, Penny asked him what this was all about.

"Well, Miss Penny. I don't rightly know how to tell you except to just say it right out. A fellow checked in at the Inn yesterday and he had some mighty strange things to say." Kane took another bite of the scone. "Dotty, you do make the best scones around. I sure do enjoy a good scone. You wouldn't happen to have a cup of coffee, would you?"

As Dotty gave Sheriff Kane a piping hot cup of coffee to go with his scone, his second scone, since the first one was already gone, she noticed Penny give her a wink.

"Well, sheriff," Penny reminded him. "What was so strange about what this guy had to say?"

"Oh, yeah .Well, he claims he is the son of Harry Powers!"

"He what!" exclaimed Penny. "What are you talking about?"

"He claims he is the son of Harry Powers!" repeated the sheriff.

Penny suddenly found that she needed to sit down. "But that's impossible! I thought his only child died. What's his name? What does he look like? How old is he?"

"He says his name is Derrick Powers, or at least that is what Joe says. I haven't talked to him yet." replied Sheriff Kane. "Joe called and told me that this guy had checked in at the Inn. When Joe saw his name was Powers, he asked if he was related to Harry or Penny Powers. Joe said the guy looked kind of funny and then he said he didn't know about Penny but Harry was his father, and then he went to his room. Boy was Joe flabbergasted! He called me right away."

"I don't know what to say either," said Penny, numb from the news.

"I know," said the sheriff. "That's why I thought before I went to check him out, that I would get a hold of you. Thought maybe you might like to go along with me when I check him out."

"I'd like that," said Penny. "When are you going?"

"Right now," relied Kane, brushing the crumbs from his mustache "Grab your jacket and come along. Joe says he's in his room yet." Kane turned and looked at Wang. "Better bring Wang along," he added.

Wang rose and went to stand at the door, waiting patiently for Penny and the sheriff.

As Sheriff Kane, Penny, and Wang drove in his cruiser to the Inn, Kane questioned Penny about her knowledge of Harry's family. "You said that Harry's child died," he said "Do you know that for a fact?"

"Yes," Penny relied. "In fact, there is an infant grave and small stone in the city cemetery. But it wasn't Derrick. I believe it was Joshua." Penny paused and was soon lost in thought.

"Earth to Penny," said the sheriff "Where'd you go off to?

"I'm sorry I was just thinking that I had not seen his wife's grave. And I wonder why it wasn't there with the baby grave."

"Well, I guess we might be finding out soon," he said as they pulled up in front of the Inn. They hurried to the office where Joe was impatiently waiting for them. "He's still in his room," Joe said. "Room 15".

The door was answered by a well-dressed young man, around Penny's age, perhaps a little older. Penny knew from her years in the city that the well-fitting clothes he wore were of top quality. "Yes?" he said as he opened the door.

"Derrick Powers?" Kane asked.

"Yes. What can I do for you?"

Kane flashed his badge "I'm Sheriff Kane. May we talk?"

The young man nodded, stepping back, "Sure, come in." As they entered the room, he looked down as Wang was sniffing at his leg.

"What's this I hear about you claiming to be the son of Harry Powers?"

Penny was jarred out of her trance. She wished the sheriff had been a little gentler about it.

"Well, I'm not just claiming to be-I am," he responded.

"But how can that be?" Penny finally joined the conversation.

Derrick Powers turned and his full attention was directed to Penny. "And I don't believe I caught your name?"

"My name is Penelope Powers," she responded "This is my dog, Wanger Doops."

"I see," Derrick said, looking at Wang still sniffing his leg "Then that explains why you and the sheriff are both here."

"Well, it doesn't explain why you are here," the sheriff exploded belligerently.

Penny gently patted the sheriff on the arm. "It's okay, Sheriff. Let's find out what he wants before you start bringing out the handcuffs."

Kane huffed into his mustache, but he stepped back and said, "Okay, Penny. Whatever you say."

"Now," said Penny "Suppose you tell us what proof you have that Harry Powers is your father."

"Won't you have a seat?" Derrick said. "I have some papers here in the desk that I can show you," he said opening the drawer. "First of all, let me explain that I didn't know that Harry was my father until just recently when my mother passed away."

"Your mother!" Penny blurted out.

"Yes. You see my mother had led me to believe that my father had died before I was born. But in her will she left me this letter explaining her deception and a safety deposit box with information about my father."

Penny was spellbound. Kane huffed again into his mustache. "Let me see that letter," Kane demanded.

While he read through it, Derrick's attention was turned to Penny. "May I ask if you are, uh, if you are, my sister?"

"No. No, I'm not," Penny replied. "Harry was my uncle. If what you are saying is true, then we are first cousins."

Kane finished reading the letter and handed it to Penny "This letter is not enough to prove that you are Harry's son," he said.

"No, maybe not. But I think with all the papers from my mother's lock box, it may be proved," he replied "You see my mother never spoke of my father. I never even knew his name."

Kane was astonished "That doesn't make sense. Why wouldn't you ask her? How could you not wonder?"

"I didn't say I didn't wonder." Derrick replied "On the contrary, I wanted to know. I tried numerous times to find out. But my mother had become a very hard woman. We did not have a good relationship at all. In fact, I was mostly raised by her aunt. When Great Aunt Mary passed on, my mother took me back, but I was just about out of high school by then and getting ready to leave home soon anyway."

As Derrick paused for breath, Penny opened the letter and began to read.

*My Dear Son,*

*If you are reading this letter, then I have departed this world. I know I have not been a good mother to you. I have not been a good person in many ways and have just recently been brought to the realization of the pain, which my path in life has caused to you.*

*I ask your forgiveness for depriving you of a father and in a way, a loving mother. Because of my disenchantment with your father, I left him and led* you to believe that he had died. I found out later that I was pregnant with you when I left him. But I chose not to tell him, or you.

I am so sorry, Derrick. If only I had realized this when you were still a little boy so that you could have known your father. But I was a bitter woman.

Two years before you were born, our first child died at birth. I very much needed the support and comfort of your father, but his business kept him from doing that and I accused him of intentionally shutting me out and blaming me for the death of our son. I realized much later when it was too late, that Harry was so depressed that he needed my support too, which I was not giving him. I am sorry, Derrick, that you never got to meet him. I wish now that things had been different. But the papers in my lock box will show you what you tried so hard to discover, who your father was and where he lived.

Please forgive me, Derrick. I love you.

Mother

Penny brushed a tear from her eye. She didn't know what to think. Was it possible that this man sitting before her was indeed her cousin? *I might have family after all.*

After perusing the papers that Derrick provided, Kane announced, "Well, at first glance, they seemed to be all in order," he told Penny. "But I would want to have them seen by a lawyer to be sure."

"Certainly," said Derrick "I too want to be sure. Tell me, is this picture the house where he lived?"

Penny took the photo he offered to her. It was indeed a picture of Burr Oak, identical to the copy that Uncle Harry had brought to the city with him. "Yes," she said weakly. "It is known as Burr Oak." She handed the picture back to him.

Eagerly he took the photo back "Does anyone live there now?" he asked.

"I do," answered Penny "It's my home now."

"Oh, that's wonderful," he said.

Kane rejoined the conversation, evidently feeling that now they were reaching the reason for Derrick coming to Gannon Ridge and that now the truth would come out. That Derrick Powers was here to claim Harry's home. "Yes! And it's going to stay her home if I have anything to say about it!"

"Why, I've no intention of changing that," Derrick said "I am simply here to discover who I am and to learn something of my father. I'm not looking to claim any of his belongings. Let me explain myself." He pulled a business card from his wallet and handed it to Penny, who showed it to Kane. The card read:

Powers Construction & Engineering

We Build You From the Ground Up

Derrick Powers, Owner & Manager

"I am very well off. I have my own business, as you can see. Two sites actually; one is on the east coast and one is on the west coast. I am not looking for any more wealth. I am merely looking to connect with my roots; for family."

Derrick looked at Wang. Penny's eyes followed his look. Suddenly, she felt good about the whole thing. Yes, this must be her cousin. Wang was all the proof she needed. For Wang was sitting next to Derrick with is head resting contentedly on Derrick's knee. You couldn't fool his nose. Wang appeared to have accepted that Derrick was indeed a Powers. He probably smelled like one.

# Chapter Twenty-five
*Epilogue – We Hear From Wang*

*Y*es siree. Can't fool this nose. Didn't take long for me to figure out that this fellow was a Powers. Smelled like one. This hound's nose has its own DNA testing and I knew after a few sniffs that Derrick Powers was related to Penny. Smelled like a really nice guy too. I could sense his honesty. Now, humans sometimes have trouble telling if someone is telling the truth or not. But not us dogs. And I could read him pretty good. Yup, Penny got herself another relative.

After living in the empty house by myself and locating the smugglers through the secret tunnel, I really think I have earned my place here.

Well, time passed and Derrick and Penny and Doc spent a lot of time together. Derrick was a busy man, but he came often to Burr Oak. He had his own plane and would just take off whenever he wanted to come out to see Penny. Sometimes he even took me up in his plane. He would let me look out the window and I would see that little French Poodle, Clarisse running around town. What a pest.

Penny, as you can imagine, was thrilled to have a relative. He's a pretty nice guy. A lot like Penny. You would never know that they hadn't grown up together. It's all in the genes, I guess. Or so I hear.

Before long, Doc and Penny's wedding rolled around. It was a big event. I expect that most of the town of Gannon Ridge was either involved in the planning of their wedding, or attending it. Doc and Penny even allowed me to have a part in it. Tried dressing me up in a tux. Well, not the whole tux; just the white collar and bow tie. Guess I did look pretty good. I checked myself out in the floor length mirror in Penny's bedroom. I did look pretty important. So I figured I'd let them have their way this one time. After all, it was for a real special occasion.

The rehearsal dinner was cool. That was my favorite part. Doc rented the Col. Tom for the evening. They even let me come and I was on my best behavior. Wedding party and guests were invited on a cruise and dinner was served by the ship's crew. Jason played piano music during the trip. Man, that guy can sure play and I like his music as long as he doesn't play that awful Wang, Wang Blues.

Penny was pretty elated at the ceremony. It was held at Burr Oak, of course. Derrick walked her down the wide Burr Oak stairway and gave her away. That sure is a funny way of saying it. Can't figure out where humans come up with some of their terms. It wasn't like he was really giving her away. Dotty and Ed were host and hostess, and Linda Booth, Bitsy and Jackie were bride's maids.

The one thing about the wedding that I didn't like was all the town kids that were there and running around, crying, getting into stuff, crying, and getting sticky stuff on my fur. Did I mention cryin'? I just don't cotton to kids. I'm a grownup's dog. Sure was glad when that was all over and I could get the sticky stuff out of my fur and the kids had all gone home. Dotty gave me a bath that night. Thank goodness! No more kids in Burr Oak! I was happy to spend my days with Doc, Penny, and Derrick.

Speaking of Derrick, I sure got to liking that fellow. He took me up in his airplane a few times. Boy, is that the way to travel. Couldn't believe the things I could see from the air. Things I had to check out once I was back on the ground. One time I spotted that Clarisse sneaking around behind the museum. She was sure up to something, I could see that. So I had to check up on her. At a distance, though. Still can't stand that yippy little mutt.

Well, in the process of checking out what Clarisse was doing, I found out that some biker bad boys, not from Gannon Ridge, were burglarizing the museum. It was a Sunday afternoon so no one would have been any the wiser if I hadn't caught them coming out the back door and raised such a ruckus that the sheriff hustled over to see what I was a howling about. Kane has turned out to be an okay sheriff. He recognizes his limitations. He confers with me on a lot of cases. 'Course, it's just between the two of us. Guess he don't want it to get out that he is relying on a dog to solve his cases. And me, well, I like working under cover. It's a good working relationship. Undercover Hound. Has a good ring to it. I had kind of enjoyed the write-up in the newspaper about my crime-solvin' capabilities. Penny read it aloud to me.

Things went on smoothly for quite a while. Penny ran the Bed & Breakfast and the gift shop. Doc still went to his clinic and treated patients during the day. Derrick dropped in for a visit every chance he could get.

One particular day, Derrick flew in and brought a big box wrapped in pretty paper. I was sniffing it out to see what it was. Derrick told me that it wasn't for me, it was for Penny and Doc, and that I could just wait and see when they opened it. Well, when they opened it, I was kind of disappointed. Looked like a small bed that rocked back and forth.

Penny said, "Wang, isn't it wonderful? Matt and I are going to have a baby!"

Man! My fur started feeling sticky already. Cryin! I could hear the crying already too. I was in for it now. I knew that babies didn't grow up as fast as puppies did. This thorn in my flesh was going to hang around for quite a while.

///////////

Ouch! Quit pulling my ear! That hurts. Get her off me! Oh, this is so humiliating.

"Mandy, mustn't pull Wang's ear. That hurts him," cautioned Penny. "Come to Mommy, sweetheart. Let's leave Wang along for a while."

Little Mandy toddled off to her mother, but only after a big squeeze around Wang's neck. Penny picked up her baby girl. "Sorry, Wang. Guess I'll have to get Mandy a big stuffed dog so she'll leave you alone."

Now wait just a cotton pickin' minute. I never said I didn't want her to hug me. Nobody's going to be replacing me, especially with some stuffed replica, and that's a fact!! Oh yeah… That's it, the left ear. Uh-huh, she's got it down right. Just like her momma.

The End

CPSIA information can be obtained
at www.ICGtesting.com
Printed in the USA
FSOW01n0234040116
15159FS